The Thief
& His Hunter

Book 3

BY

Eidahs

Cover & Editing by
Binky Ink

Binky Ink

The literary arm of Binky Productions

www.binkyproductions.com/TheThiefandHisHunter

TABLE OF CONTENTS

'This is an item I retrieved for a client.' said Conor. He recognised the clip drive immediately. 'It was legit stolen from them.'

An Asian man had approached Conor, claiming to represent a client, and had brought the receipts Conor needed to prove the clip drive belonged to their organisation, whatever that was. At the time, Conor thought nothing more of it. Now he realised he must have been dealing with mobsters who were this Yakuza man's rivals.

'Except that person first stole what belonged to *me*. Before we could track our quarry down here, he moved back to Osaka and is conducting his business there again. We want you to help us retrieve this clip drive from this person.'

'Wait, you expect us to agree to go to Japan with you for this?' Theron pointed at the Yakuza, 'Why can't *you* get it yourselves? You seem well resourced.'

'Our faces are too recognisable, Mister Morin, as I'm certain you understand. Plus, entering the facility requires more . . . unique skills, the kind of which Vulpis possesses.'

Conor exhaled slowly through his nose, still staring at the image. 'I'm sorry. I can't help you.'

'We're not asking.' The man placed his hand on his pistol, while the other unclipped a taser.

Conor clenched his jaw and swallowed hard, exchanging a furtive glance with Theron.

'Now, you can either come with us willingly and enjoy the luxuries of my private jet. Or . . . we can take you by force.'

CHAPTER 1

Present Moment.

Theron and Conor sat in the private jet as it flew above the world – destination: Osaka, Japan.

Theron harrumphed, crossing his arms. The seats were luxurious, everything was above and beyond what First Class could ever offer, and yet, the fact that they sat facing two armed mafia men prevented Theron from enjoying the flight.

Conor, who sat beside him, was scrolling through images on Theron's phone – the thief, as per, had left his at home. 'Oh, look, there she is looking like the cutie she is.'

'Mmhmm,' Theron answered absent-mindedly, as he glowered at his . . . What, captors? They weren't bound, but . . .

'Babe, you're not even looking.'

'Huh?' Theron turned his head to Conor.

The thief waved the phone about. 'Fidelis, all adorable, playing with Barry.'

'Sorry if I can't appreciate it when we're literally sitting in front of two mobsters who forced us on this plane with them.'

Conor sighed. He glanced at the leader. 'Honestly, I appreciate you letting me stop by home to grab my gear and say a temporary goodbye to my dog.'

The man with the longer face, who seemed to be in charge, smirked, looking entertained. 'I did not realise Vulpis had so many copies of his armour.'

'Ooh, armour. Did you hear that, babe?' Conor nudged Theron with his shoulder.

'How are you this excitable?'

'Theron. The guy put his hand on his gun. Neither of them ever actually threatened us at gunpoint.'

The man had certainly made his point and gotten their 'cooperation.' And yet, he *had* allowed them to stop by home. Still, they were mobsters, and that made them lawbreakers.

Theron narrowed his eyes. 'Not even halfway there and you're suffering from Stockholm syndrome.'

Conor rolled his eyes. 'I am making the best of our situation.'

'That's because you're reckless. *I* prefer to remain cautious.'

'As do we.' Their host looked more than amused. 'Do keep in mind that we are aware your dogsitter is your former detective partner, Mister Morin, and that we have long since flown out of American air. Anything he may relay to your former boss will do nothing to change your situation or save you from it.'

Theron just scowled harder in response.

Conor put the phone away. 'Maybe it would help if you told us your names, now that we are in the air, away from home. I need to build trust with my clients.'

'Of course. I would also like to establish trust with you, as well as establish the finer details of our agreement.'

'Agreement is a generous word,' Theron muttered under his breath.

'While we will not be paying you until the job is complete,' their Japanese host went on, 'you will be lodged, and equipped with the necessary.'

'You mean guns.' Theron huffed and sighed.

'All right.' The man stood and bowed curtly from the waist. Theron recognised the show of respect. The Japanese man sat back down. 'Kiyoshi Tachibana. Yakuza leader of Tachibana Clan in the Osaka prefecture.' He pointed his thumb at his compatriot. 'And my bodyguard and trusted friend, Aritomo-san.'

Theron nodded in acknowledgement, while Conor held out his hand.

'Vulpis. You can call me Conor.'

They shook hands.

'I can't believe you're actually enjoying yourself,' muttered Theron. 'Honestly, you're so reckless.'

'Stickler,' Conor muttered back without even looking at Theron.

Kiyoshi chuckled.

'So . . . there's something I've been trying to make sense of since we took flight,' began Conor, adopting a comfortable pose in his seat. 'Because you said the guy with the clip drive first took something from you.' Conor pointed behind him. 'That clip drive had a receipt. From a long time ago. Honestly, I was surprised his people still had his receipt.'

'It is not the clip drive that belongs to us.'

'What!' exclaimed Theron.

'But what it contains.'

'Wait,' said Conor. 'Ohhh, so the clip drive has *information* that's yours.'

'You never investigated the drive?' Kiyoshi inquired, quirking an eyebrow.

'I don't pry,' replied Conor. 'But a drive with info on enemy mobsters . . . well, I guess that explains his urgency to have it retrieved.'

Theron was confused. 'If he has info on you, then isn't it too late to erase that?'

'You don't understand, Mister Morin. It is not *what* is on the drive that is mine, but the information will lead to what *is*.'

'I'm not following.'

Kiyoshi stood and crossed the aisle to stare out the window at the bright sun as they flew high above the clouds. The warm light cast an orange glow on his bronze face.

'I am searching for a woman. The information on the drive will lead me to her.'

'How do you know this?' asked Conor.

Kiyoshi, his back to them, explained. 'The man, Shibuya, took something from me a long time ago, and that clip drive is the key to finding . . . her. Shibuya is a rival of the Yakuza and leads a mafia called *Nesshün'na Kōkan* – Diligent Exchange.' Kiyoshi balled his hands into fists and his voice grew rough. 'He is a human slave trafficker.'

Something hit Theron in the pit of his stomach. 'Shit. And Shibuya took that woman from you.' He raised his voice. 'Oh my god, you're into human slave trafficking too, aren't you?'

Kiyoshi looked back over his shoulder. 'Think what you want, Mister Morin. I will not waste my breath on meaningless drivel or arguments.'

'Wait,' Conor said gently. He placed his hand on Theron's arm. 'I don't think that's what it is.' He looked up at Kiyoshi. 'Who is this woman to you?'

Kiyoshi faced them anew, his face deceiving his grief. 'She is my sister.'

Theron's stomach clenched, and the reality of it all hit him like a punch in the gut. 'Shit. I'm sorry.'

Theron had misjudged the situation. Sure, he had his judgements – and reservations – but this man, despite being a mafia boss in his prefecture, was looking for his sister. And the way he felt about what Shibuya did for a living told Theron that Kiyoshi had enough of a conscience to be against acts as vile as human slave trafficking.

Kiyoshi returned to his seat. He folded a leg, resting his ankle on his knee. 'The *Nesshīn'na Kōkan* attacked the Yakuza one night and took Azumi-san, my sister, from us. Just like they took many girls from many regions. That is the night they killed my father.'

Kiyoshi's eyes grew distant for a moment, as though he were reliving the events of that night.

'I am the eldest of three children. I was too young to take over from my father then. My brother and I have been searching for my sister ever since. It has been . . . twenty years. She was 13. I was 15.'

Theron and Conor exchanged a glance, smiling in sympathy.

'Yeah, we know what it's like to be searching for someone, sort of, for that long,' Conor said gently. 'Not the same, of course, but . . .'

'Then you understand the . . .' Kiyoshi searched for the word. He put a hand to the centre of his chest.

'Yeah, it grips you and . . . consumes you,' said Conor.

'That is why I need your services, Vulpis.'

Conor nodded slowly. 'So the clip drive must contain records of all the girls this guy has been trafficking over the years, where they were last, and if—' He stopped abruptly. 'Sorry.'

'If they were ever sold or killed,' completed Kiyoshi. He sighed, leaning back, head resting against the head-rest as he gazed towards the far window.

'I'll get that clip drive,' asserted Conor. 'And we'll find your sister.'

Kiyoshi offered him a mild smile in thanks before the four men fell silent.

<CENTER><H1>CHAPTER 2</H1></CENTER>

The private jet touched down on the landing pad of the Osaka airport. When they stepped out, the air was crisp, and snow still speckled the ground, though there was a warmth to the sun, and the burgeoning leaves of the cherry blossoms indicated that the warm days of spring in Japan were on their way.

A limousine took the four men to a district called Umeda.

A wide busy boulevard curved towards tall complexes. A shopping mall that looked like a sports centre had a large sign that flashed with rotating images. A hotel whose windows looked silver loomed above as they drove past. Conor also clocked several bars along the way. Japanese folks in business attire walked with hurried steps, while others slowed and meandered along side-alleys, carrying their shopping into their apartments.

It wasn't long before they entered a lavish building with a fountain in the lobby that jetted up several storeys. Conor and Theron followed Kiyoshi and Aritomo up the elevator.

'He still could've explained all that *before* threatening us back home,' Theron complained as the two of them were led into a fancy apartment Conor guessed served as a safehouse of sorts.

'You know I can hear you, Mister Morin,' said Kiyoshi. Theron rolled his eyes. Conor suppressed a chuckle.

Kiyoshi motioned with an open palm towards one of the bedrooms and the two husbands entered the room. Theron dumped his suitcase on the bed with a wide arc of his arm, and signed.

Conor came to stand behind him, wrapping his arms around him from under his arms. 'Hey,' he whispered gently, kissing Theron's nape and feeling his husband's warmth, 'look at this as the honeymoon trip we never got to go on.'

Theron smiled. 'Except our honeymoon wouldn't involve Vulpis jobs or guns or mafia or—'

Conor turned Theron's face to meet his gaze and kissed him to stop his enumeration, a long tender kiss he had longed for during the entire flight here.

Theron moaned softly. 'Mmmm.' Smiling, the detective deepened the kiss, turning and wrapping his arms around Conor. 'Almost made me forget the Vulpis job and guns and mafia and—'

'Oh my god, Theron!' Conor leaned back on his heels while holding onto Theron. 'Take a breath. We'll be okay.'

Theron's eyebrows drew together in concern. As he spoke, he passed the back of his fingers over Conor's cheek. 'I just worry about you, darling.'

'I know, babe. I can be reckless.'

Theron sighed. 'Maybe I am just too much of a stickler to let go and enjoy this trip despite our circumstances.'

'I'll have my hunter protecting me.' Biting his lower lip flirtatiously, Conor looped his arms around Theron's neck.

'And my thief will keep me on my toes.'

Conor leaned forward and kissed Theron again, relishing this small moment they had. 'I love you,' he said with tenderness.

Theron smiled softly. 'I love you.'

'Now, let's not keep our host waiting any longer, but tonight,' he leaned forward and whispered in Theron's ear, excited at the prospect, 'I'm going to treat this like a vacation and help you forget everything else.'

Theron's hold on Conor tightened and he shuddered a breath. He kept Conor from pulling away. 'Conor, you can't do that. Turn me on when we can't follow through.'

Giggling, Conor led Theron by the hand to the common room.

'I have to meet with my man underground,' Kiyoshi announced. 'And gather some Intel. Aritomo-san will keep guard, but please, make yourselves comfortable. I will return in an hour or so.'

Conor arched his brow at Theron, his smile quickly growing into a grin. He saw the relief, tension, *and* arousal on Theron's face.

'Take your time,' Conor told Kiyoshi. 'We'll take a nap.'

Kiyoshi made one of those faces that said he knew what kind of 'nap' Conor meant.

Giggling silly, with a hand on his husband's chest, Conor ushered Theron back into the room. He shut the door with his back, pulling Theron to him for a fiery kiss that had his whole body tingling, as always.

Theron pressed his forehead to Conor's. He whispered, 'Oh my god, Conor, you're so reckless. This is so—'

Conor didn't let him finish. He claimed his lips once more. Theron's grip became possessive as he pressed himself to him. It took Conor's breath away. He pulled back, lips lingering close.

Conor bit his lower lip, desiring Theron just as much as always. Theron's face betrayed uncertainty still, despite his heaving chest.

Conor instructed gently, 'Just relax and forget all that.'

Theron's eyes darkened with desire and his voice grew husky, sending a thrill through Conor's body. 'Then make love to me and *make sure* I forget all that.'

Grinning, Conor obliged, and he took tender care of Theron so his mind was blank and on him right now, and only him.

* * *

When the two husbands emerged from the room, cleaned up and satiated, Kiyoshi was stepping into the apartment. He was all-business as he spoke authoritatively to Aritomo who nodded and left the safehouse.

Their host turned to the two Americans. 'I trust you rested well?'

Theron felt himself blush and averted his eyes. He glanced at Conor who was grinning far too much and letting on far too much to Theron's liking. It made Theron's face feel even hotter.

Kiyoshi, to no avail, suppressed a smile before chuckling. 'I see. I am pleased to know you have made yourselves . . . more comfortable in my country.'

'Oh my god,' Theron breathed out, his voice barely audible. His heart was thudding so hard, he was certain both Conor and Kiyoshi could hear it. And he was certain Conor was doing it on purpose to make Theron feel even more self-conscious. His husband could be so reckless sometimes.

Conor pressed his teeth on his tongue as he grinned at Theron. 'We did get *some* rest in, didn't we, babe? What with how spent we were—'

Theron had had enough. Theron motioned his hands emphatically as he turned to Conor. 'Oh my god, Conor, can you please? Not embarrass us in front of strangers? Mafia on top of that!'

'Embarrass?' Conor's face fell.

Theron felt a pang. 'Darling, not in *that* sense.'

'We're husbands, Theron. I'm not going to hide how we are with each other just because.'

'I know. I just mean . . . It's neither the time nor place nor the person for us to be playful with each other in front of.'

The whole time, Kiyoshi stared at them, an eyebrow raised, listening to their exchange.

Conor lowered his voice, asserting himself in a tone that always tingled Theron's senses in every way. 'I'm not going to suppress what we share just because of our circumstances. I don't care where we are and who is with us. You're my husband and I'm going to act with you how I've always acted.'

'Conor,' Theron warned. 'We don't act a certain way in public, and in Japan couples do even less, so . . .'

'We are not in public,' Conor argued teasingly.

Theron widened his eyes. He whisper-shouted, his jaw clenched. 'We are in the presence of a Japanese mafia mob boss.'

'Yes,' said Kiyoshi, 'and this "Japanese mafia mob boss" is highly amused by your exchange.'

Conor slumped his shoulders. 'I just don't understand why you'd want me to act any differently than at any other time.'

That tugged on Theron's heart, and reassuring Conor became a priority over acting a certain way in front of their Japanese mobster host slash kidnapper.

Theron sighed. 'I guess I'm just stressed and worried because of everything.' He took Conor's hand. 'Darling, you know I love it when you show me affection.' Theron cursed himself for insinuating otherwise and for making Conor feel bad.

The truth was he *was* stressed and worried, and hyper-vigilant. They had never hidden their affection in front of others before. Granted they played to the decorum of being in public when they were, but Theron realised he was acting as though he were undercover.

Kiyoshi, for his part, stepped aside and made a quick phone call before returning to the husbands.

Conor kissed Theron's cheek. 'I know. You're so tense. Just . . . *try* to relax.'

Theron looked at Kiyoshi who was now texting away on his phone. 'Do *you* get into silly arguments with *your* spouse?'

'Silly!' exclaimed Conor, feigning dejection with a hand over his heart.

'I do not have a spouse,' Kiyoshi answered dryly. He nodded. 'When you are ready . . .'

Theron straightened. 'We're ready.'

'Good. The clip drive is at the *Nesshiin'na Kōkan* headquarters. Someone who knows the headquarters' location will be attending a V.I.P. event at a club in the Dotonbori neighbourhood. I will need you both to get familiar with the surroundings before this event.'

'You mean you want me to be able to travel roof-to-roof,' Conor deduced.

'Correct. I will require you to remain on the roof and keep an eye out for anything suspicious.'

'Like anyone from the enemy faction,' said Conor. Kiyoshi nodded.

'And once we're in, how will we get the information we need?' asked Theron.

The look on Kiyoshi's face sent a chill running down his spine.

'I will question my target.'

Theron swallowed. 'When you say question, you mean torture, don't you?' Kiyoshi needn't confirm verbally, the fiery look in his eyes said it all. 'Good thing we'll be on the roof, then.'

'The roof is made of glass,' added Kiyoshi.

'Then I'll just look away.'

Kiyoshi tilted his head up, looking down from his nose. 'I understand your reservations to my methods, Mister Morin, but please remember we are after a slave trafficker.'

Conor gently squeezed Theron's hand, sending re-assurance.

'I also need Vulpis to enter the club from the roof should anything go wrong. I trust that shouldn't be a problem.'

'Not in the slightest,' Conor confirmed.

Theron knew their Japanese associate wasn't sharing everything, but he found himself foolishly hoping they wouldn't run into any nasty surprises.

'Are you expecting trouble?' asked Theron.

'I am *Yakuza*. I always expect trouble.'

Theron shifted uneasily.

'I hope you are rested, because I need you fit. We begin the exploration of the neighbourhood rooftops tonight.'

<u>CHAPTER 3</u>

Dotonbori was bustling with people and teeming with the energy only clubgoers exuded. Flashing signs, neon lights, effervescent colours, all illuminating the night. Music reverberated through the clubs' walls.

A canal passed between two walkways with bridges that connected the two sides. Small boats passed along, where tourists, friends, and lovers alike enjoyed the slow pace that contrasted the fast-changing lights and beats.

Along the streets, food stands offered an array of delicacies, from authentic Japanese foods to European snacks. The smells that wafted to Theron's nose made him crave a snack, before he reminded himself they were here on a mission and to get the lay of the land, not to enjoy a night out.

There was a building where Kiyoshi dropped the pair off. Conor and Theron made their way to the top floor via the elevator – a fancy white-walled elevator – then found the emergency stairwell and reached the roof. From there, Conor studied the area.

'I've never scaled a skyscraper before,' he had told Kiyoshi before leaving, and Kiyoshi explained the plan.

On the first night of parkouring Dotonbori, they didn't get very far.

'I'm going to need a grappling hook,' Conor announced, and he alluded to some safety measures he ensured when rock climbing.

So the following day, Conor was granted a grappling hook. The husbands were also each given guns and holsters. Theron wasn't sure how he felt about wielding a gun again, especially under such illegal circumstances. Only a few months without one and the feel of a pistol now weighed heavily on his conscience. Then again, he was well-trained and knew he could better protect Conor this way, even if Conor had his own gun too.

Several nights later, it was the V.I.P. event and they were ready to move in.

* * *

Kiyoshi had set them up with earpieces that were linked via the network from his laptop back at the safehouse. To ensure complete surprise, only the four of them – Kiyoshi, Aritomo, Theron and Conor – knew about the operation.

Kiyoshi confirmed Aritomo was in position as backup outside the club proper as Kiyoshi entered the club. The roof vibrated with the pounding of the loud music within, music that was muffled where Conor and Theron stood.

They made their way to the section of the club's roof vis-à-vis the private rooms. The glass roof provided an overview of many such rooms.

Conor peered down and saw Kiyoshi enter a private lounge where sat a man surrounded by young women. He wondered if any of them had been trafficked and if their flirtatiousness with him was consensual or if they had been coerced into being his dates.

A look of disdain from Theron told Conor he was wondering the same thing.

Conor and Theron kept to the shadows, hidden by some beams. They couldn't understand the words Kiyoshi was saying, but the authoritative tone he used, the menace in his voice that had the women scattering away from the lounge, and the fear in the other man's voice, told them enough.

Kiyoshi raised his gun and the other man raised his arms in surrender. Kiyoshi waved the gun, giving a curt reply. Conor guessed he gave the man an order, for this one stood and turned around. Kyoshi then handcuffed him and turned him back around, sat him back down, and cuffed his legs.

Kiyoshi crouched, pressing his gun to the man's chin as he took out a knife. He turned the knife around as he spoke at length before pressing it just beneath the man's eye.

Conor couldn't watch anymore.

Theron's lips were pressed in a thin line. He looked like he was going to puke.

'It's okay,' Conor whispered.

Theron shook his head. 'This isn't right. This isn't how this should be approached.'

'What would you suggest, then?' Conor waited for Theron's reply. Their earpieces grew quiet.

'Don't tell me you agree with this!' Theron hissed.

'No, I don't – but I get it. This isn't our jurisdiction. This is how the Yakuza deal with this, with such people. I'm just adapting. I want to go back home as much as you do, but I won't let what's happening change me, change how I am with you, or change—'

Something about the quiet felt off. Conor suddenly stopped, tapping his earpiece. Theron scowled, tapping his own, as though he too heard the small pop in his ears.

Conor peered down. Kiyoshi was shouting at his whimpering captive, evident from the wide mouth articulation and arm gestures, but nothing was coming through their earpieces.

'Something's not right,' said Theron. He glanced around, moving from their spot to another area of the roof. 'Shit!'

Conor looked up to see a shadow cross Theron's face as he stared down at something beneath him.

'Conor?'

The tremble in Theron's voice hit Conor's stomach with a cold sensation. Conor dashed to Theron's side and followed his gaze down to the adjacent V.I.P. room. Empty, except for one bomb, with blinking lights, lots of wires, and a counter that indicated only fifteen minutes remained.

Conor clenched his jaw as fear struck him. He stared at Theron who met his gaze, terror in his eyes.

'We have to get out of here now,' Theron whispered a panicked command.

'What about Kiyoshi?' Conor asked in alarm.

'Our kidnapper?' Theron's voice was shrill. 'Forget him. Let's just run to safety while we still can.'

Conor pressed his lips together, sucking them in as he thought for a quick beat. This didn't feel right – to abandon their only guide, to let someone die. It went against Conor's values. He shook his head. The crease of Theron's brows told Conor his husband understood, even if he didn't like it.

Conor glanced down – thirteen minutes.

He sprang towards the glass above the other lounge.

'Conor, what are you doing?'

Conor positioned himself to stand just above the man Kiyoshi was questioning and got down on his knees. He began slicing through the glass with his stainless steel card-knife. It offered little resistance if Conor went with hard strokes, which alleviated some of his panic.

'Conor!'

'Theron, get beside me. On your knees or in a crouch to cushion your fall.'

'Oh my fucking god, you're so fucking reckless!' argued Theron, but he joined Conor as the thief cut the glass clean.

They fell through, dropping atop the captive and knocking him unconscious. Kiyoshi glanced up just before they crashed down and the glass shattered on the other man's head.

Kiyoshi jumped back, crying out in surprise and confusion.

'Cover Kiyoshi!' shouted Conor, flipping the knife's protector over with a flick of his wrist. 'I'll get the bomb!'

'What! No! Conor!'

His next tool already in hand, Conor darted out of the V.I.P. room and to the next one as he pocketed his card-knife. He began lockpicking his way into the locked room. He was so nervous and pressed for time, he fumbled for a second even if he was an expert lockpicker. Clammy fingers sticking out of his tactical flip-top gloves, Conor took a deep breath to go slowly, despite his racing heart, so he would succeed the first time and quickly.

Click. He was through. Conor let out a breath and wiped the sweat from his brow, his brain already onto the next step.

Racing into the room, he readied his grappling hook as he snatched the bomb, carrying it under his arm like he would carry Fidelis when she was a pup.

He scored the glass with his cutter and kicked the window through. The glass shattered to the floor, large chunks of it falling out into the night. After securing his grappling hook, ensuring it latched onto the window frame, Conor backed a few steps before running, giving himself momentum, and lunged out of the building, tossing the bomb as far and high into the air as he possibly could.

Conor's stomach lurched in that moment of near free-fall, right before the grappling hook yanked Conor back towards the club, his stomach rising to his throat.

He slammed against the wall beneath the broken window. He climbed the rope and lifted himself back onto the floor. Yanking the grappling hook back to him and rolling it back into its harness, Conor ran to the other V.I.P. where Theron was shouting at Kiyoshi, panicked, as the mobster shouted back trying to understand what was going on over the din of the music.

'Move!' shouted Conor. 'We need to get out of here!'

He grabbed Theron's hand and instinctively interlaced their fingers as Theron reflexively opened his arms protectively to shield Kiyoshi just as the bomb outside the other side of the club went off.

The building shook, the walls exploded, and the air propelled them out of the window, crashing through the breaking glass and out into the night.

Conor's heart nearly stopped as the three of them held onto each other, their bodies flying out from the blast. Suspended between forward momentum and falling, Conor looked down to see the canal, wondering how deep it was and if they could survive a plunge from this high up.

He twirled his wrist and sent his grappling hook to the nearest building's fixtures.

The three men slammed against the wall, bruised but alive.

Panting, Conor looked down and behind him. They had fallen many storeys in their flight.

'When I give the go, we kick off the wall and let go.' He began detaching the hook's harness. 'One, two, three.' He let 'Go!'

The three men kicked off the wall, Theron and Kiyoshi following Conor's instruction without argument, letting go of the rope from the grappling hook and of each other.

Arms and legs flailing, they descended into the canal. Conor took in a large intake of air before hitting the water. He swore he touched the bottom of the canal as the plunge took him deep under the water. He kicked up, swimming to the surface where he heard the other two inhale loudly.

Heart racing, Conor met Theron's eyes as his husband swam towards him, took his hand, and pulled Conor to him, wrapping one arm around him in a protective embrace as the other paddled to keep them afloat. Even if Theron's face was wet, Conor recognised the stream of tears running down his face.

Kiyoshi gaped at the two men, working his jaw. Finally, he exclaimed in an almost whisper, 'You saved my life!'

CHAPTER 4

'What the hell happened?' demanded Theron as they climbed out of the canal, soaked from head to toe. He looked around. Thankfully the nightlife was subdued here to where they had swum. Aside from a few on-lookers, they were alone.

'Whoever planted that bomb must think we're dead,' voiced Conor, his wet hair plastered to his face.

'Good!' Kiyoshi's face contorted as he marched away from the canal, water dripping from his clothes.

'Who else knew about this operation?' asked Theron, following close behind.

'No one.'

'Then what happened?' asked Conor.

'I was betrayed.' Kiyoshi stopped and spun to face the two husbands. 'Aritomo.' His features betrayed a whirlwind of emotions. Theron clocked the lack of suffix Kiyoshi had previously used when speaking of and addressing his bodyguard. 'He was my oldest friend.' Kiyoshi started off again. 'We need to get to a safehouse

Aritomo knows nothing about. I need to get in touch with my man underground.'

Theron and Conor caught up to walk side by side with Kiyoshi.

'Who's your man underground?' asked Theron.

'My brother. Takuto-san.'

Drenched and cold, Theron and Conor followed Kiyoshi to a forlorn district and into a building whose safe-house apartment was simple and sparsely furnished.

They found some clothes to change into while their other garments dried.

Kiyoshi had remained silent the whole way, aside from a few quick and sharp words to indicate the place or instructions.

The mafia clan leader opened a small cabinet and pulled out a bottle of saké. Theron recognised the details on the bottle – green with golden letters – from a brewery that exported to America. Kiyoshi took out three small *o-choko* cups and sat down on the leather couch. He was still seething.

Kiyoshi poured the saké into the three cups, chuckling mirthlessly to himself. Theron and Conor joined him, sitting in the armchairs that faced the couch.

'I have to thank you for saving my life.' Kiyoshi lifted his cup in salute. Then, with care, placed the other two in front of each of his wards.

Theron hesitated. 'It was all Conor. I wanted to run and save my skin,' he admitted.

'Theron found the bomb,' Conor interjected quickly. 'Else we'd *all* have been . . .' He pressed his lips together and his eyes sparkled.

Theron placed his hand in Conor's as it sank in. By finding the bomb, he saved Conor's life too. Had he not, he and Conor would have died from that blast.

'It is normal to want to save your life above others,' voiced Kiyoshi. 'I hold no grudge against you for that.' He eyed the two men. 'Your recklessness served me well tonight, Vulpis. As did your skills as a detective, Mister Morin.' Kiyoshi gestured with his cup to each of them.

Theron and Conor lifted their cups and nodded before the three of them took a sip.

'So much for trying to find the location of the H.Q. with the clip drive,' muttered Conor.

'Ah, but I got the information I sought in the end, just before you descended upon us.' Kiyoshi smirked in satisfaction. 'And I needn't even cut my victim, only graze him enough to frighten him into talking. That is why I targeted him. He was weak enough to break easily.'

'I guess that's good news,' said Theron, unsure if he was too shocked to feel disdain or if he was more neutral about it.

Kiyoshi leaned back against the couch, chuckling to himself. His chuckle was sporadic before it turned into a laugh that lasted a good long minute, as he tilted his head up towards the ceiling. He exhaled, his gaze falling back on the men before him.

'The two men I can trust the most right now, are the ones I forcefully coerced into this job.' He shook his head before taking another sip of saké.

Kiyoshi pointed a finger at them from the hand holding the cup at his mouth. 'Two *white* men at that, and gay. This goes against all Yakuza tradition, and right now, I don't care.' He lowered his voice, muttering, 'I was never one for following tradition explicitly anyway.'

Kiyoshi breathed out another small laugh, shaking his head before taking another sip.

Theron and Conor exchanged a furtive glance, smiling in sympathy.

'It has been one hell of a night, hasn't it? Even for me,' Conor said gently.

Kiyoshi sobered and slammed his cup down on the small coffee table. He stood and met Theron's and Conor's eyes, conviction on his face and in his voice.

'I owe you for saving my life. You did not have to risk your lives for me and yet you did.' He muttered something in Japanese before bowing low from the waist, his eyes always locked on them. He held the bow this time. 'Thank you, *Theron.*' He paused deliberately. 'Thank you, *Conor.*' He emphasised their first names.

It was the first time Theron heard Kiyoshi speak their names like that, and it moved him. He turned his head to Conor who looked awed.

Conor stood first, setting his cup down, and bowed from the waist like the Japanese man had. Theron followed suit, his heart filling with warmth he did not expect to feel for this mobster when he first met him, now feeling the respect Kiyoshi was showing them and the gratitude he was trying to convey.

The three men nodded and rose. They sat back down and downed the rest of their saké. There was nothing left to say.

* * *

Kiyoshi had taken the couch to sleep while Theron and Conor had the bed in the only bedroom there was. Conor kept complaining he was cold.

Theron got up as morning came, yawning. He checked his clothes. They were dry by now, so he dressed in his attire, setting the borrowed garments aside.

Kiyoshi stood in the kitchenette, preparing some tea. 'Good morning, Theron.'

'Morning, Kiyoshi.'

Theron sat on the stool at the kitchenette counter. Kiyoshi remained on the other side. The Japanese man offered Theron some tea and Theron accepted.

Kiyoshi observed him, a smile tugging on the corner of his mouth. 'You and your husband are very affectionate with each other. You love each other very much, yes?'

Theron smiled, blushing. 'He drives me nuts, but he's the love of my life.'

Kiyoshi grinned knowingly. 'You've known him a long time?'

'Since we were five,' replied Theron. Kiyoshi's eyes widened. 'Conor moved away at fifteen and I was stupid and got us into a big fight for nothing. We hadn't seen each other for fifteen years. I was hunting Vulpis, and, well . . .'

Theron felt flutters in his stomach, just remembering seeing Conor for the first time after fifteen years, remembering their love declarations, the way Conor acted with him, and the thrill despite the frustrations.

'We knew right away we loved each other. We declared our love and it drove me insane.'

Theron tapped his index on the counter. 'I searched the law for a loophole so that Conor wouldn't go to jail, so that we could be together. And he made the necessary compromises – for me.'

'That is adorable. Admirable.'

'How about you? You said you have no spouse.'

'No,' sighed Kiyoshi. 'She would either have to be Yakuza, know little and be okay with what I do, or know nothing at all.'

'Gotcha.'

'It is difficult in my line of work to settle down and have a family. My father was fortunate.'

'And your mother?'

Kiyoshi smiled fondly. 'She continued to raise Takuto-san and me until we were old enough. Then we got her out of Osaka. She has moved around a bit and communicates with us seldom but enough for us to know she is safe.'

'I understand.' Theron considered the man. 'I suppose you're not all bad. I mean, I don't agree with your methods, but . . . I don't know. Last night, despite my initial impulse to just run for my life, I'm glad we saved your life. I'm glad Conor was reckless.'

'You balance each other out,' observed Kiyoshi, the response an acknowledgement to Theron's declaration.

'That, we do.' Theron felt a tender tug at his heart. He took a sip of his tea.

A moan of complaint came from the bedroom. Theron furrowed his brows, standing. 'Conor?' He entered the room, Kiyoshi behind him.

Conor was tossing in bed, his face had a faded pallor and sickly sheen to it. Theron hurried to Conor's side, sitting on the edge of the bed, and pressed his hand to Conor's forehead. 'Oh my god, darling, you're burning up.'

Kiyoshi slid open a closet and took out a thick blanket, placing it over Conor on top of the other covers. He hurried out of the room and returned a moment later with a cool wet cloth, placing it on Conor's forehead.

Theron gently moved some stray hairs from Conor's face as Conor moaned again but nestled into Theron as he turned to his side.

'You'll be all right, darling.' Theron bent and kissed Conor's temple.

'He must've caught cold when we left the canal,' said Kiyoshi, stating the obvious in a reassuring tone.

Theron nodded, wrapping his arms around Conor.

Aside from idle chit-chat with Kiyoshi and eating from time to time, Theron remained by Conor's side. Kiyoshi sat in the armchair beside the bed while chatting with Theron who lay beside Conor, holding his husband. That is where they fell asleep that night.

A loud thud jolted Theron awake. He looked about. He heard something again. He rolled over towards Kiyoshi and nudged the man's knee with his hand.

He whispered, 'Hey, Kiyoshi!'

Kiyoshi groaned awake, opening his groggy eyes.

'Is that normal?' Theron asked as his heart began to race.

Kiyoshi listened. The sound came again and the mobster's eyes widened. His whisper was panicked. 'They've found us!'

Theron was packing the little they had – the Vulpis outfit, their guns, Conor's accessories – into a small backpack and placed it on his back.

He shook Conor. 'Conor, darling, wake up.'

Conor merely moaned in response, his brows knit together as sweat added to the feverish glow of his face.

'Shit, he's out cold.'

Kiyoshi secured his gun, the click as he loaded the magazine sending jolts of fear through Theron. The mafia boss snuck a peek through the drapes then verified the door was clear, then returned.

'They've surrounded the building but they have not entered. We can make our way to the back.' He pulled out his phone, dialling.

'Who are you calling?'

'My brother. I did not tell him our location previously in case they found and questioned him.' Theron understood the implications. If any of them were captured and tortured, the less they knew, the better for the others.

Kiyoshi began talking quickly in Japanese over the phone, his voice a hushed but harsh whisper.

Theron tossed the covers aside, then wrapped Conor in the thick blanket. He scooped him up, carrying him as he held him close to his chest.

Kiyoshi beckoned Theron to follow, gun held at the ready.

They made their way down the hall, scurrying quietly. When they reached the door at the back, Kiyoshi stopped.

'Wait here. I will clear our way.'

Kiyoshi waited just long enough to get confirmation through a chime on his phone. Then the clan leader yanked the door open and began shooting the mobsters outside left and right. Conor shuddered at the noise. Theron held him evermore protectively.

Gunshots rang in the night. Theron pressed himself against the opposite wall, shutting his eyes tight, wishing they were back home with Fidelis.

Tires screeched, and shortly after, the gunshots ceased. Kiyoshi shouted. 'Theron-san!'

It took Theron a beat to register before he bolted out of the building, pressing Conor to his chest. The door at the back of a sleek black car was open and Theron lunged in. Kiyoshi was shooting again, shutting the rear door and covering Theron and Conor before getting into the passenger seat and slamming the door shut as the car sped off.

The man driving blurted in Japanese and Kiyoshi answered in kind.

Kiyoshi looked back at Theron. 'Theron-san, how is Conor-san?'

'Uh, he's still out of it, but he's unharmed, as far as I can tell. We're both unharmed. Thank you.'

After a few tense moments of speeding and swerving, the car slowed just a little.

'We'll be driving out of Osaka to stay low for a while,' explained Kiyoshi. 'To ensure the *Nesshiin'na Kōkan* cannot follow or find us again.'

'Are we certain that you can trust the rest of your people?' Theron asked, surprised at his own concern for Kiyoshi.

'Yes. Takuto-san was very thorough in his questioning after apprehending our betrayer. Aritomo was their man on the inside.'

Theron acknowledged Takuto who nodded to Theron, meeting his eyes through the rearview mirror.

Then Theron realised the meaning behind Kiyoshi's words. He swallowed hard. 'Was. Aritomo is dead?'

Kiyoshi pressed his lips together and returned to face front, his silence giving Theron his answer.

* * *

The car ride was long, and Theron was beginning to worry about Conor more and more – he was burning up and murmuring in his sleep. Conor lay atop Theron's lap as the detective cradled him.

Theron stroked Conor's cheek, soothing him. 'It's okay, darling. We're safe.'

'I don't want to leave you,' Conor mumbled.

Theron furrowed his brows.

'Our friendship means everything to me.'

Theron froze. He surmised Conor must be dreaming about their past, and it broke his heart.

'Why are you saying these things?' Conor wept feverishly, a stray tear trickling down the side of his temple. Theron wiped it gently with his thumb.

'Darling, it's okay. I'm right here.' Theron rocked Conor in his arms.

'Mmmm, Theron. Please don't hate me.'

'I *love* you, Conor.'

Theron held Conor closer to him, pressing his lips together in worry. Conor's murmurs brought Theron right back to their past.

* * *

Conor approached looking solemn. 'So, like, I'm moving across the country.'

Theron felt a sharp pain in his heart. 'What?'

'My dad has a contract there.' Conor averted his gaze. He bit his lower lip. 'Wish I could bring you with me.'

Theron reached for Conor's face with a hand and then dropped it. 'When?'

Conor shrugged. 'His contract starts right away, so we're moving next week – that's what my mom said. It's a shock, but . . .' Emotions warred on his face. Then he grinned. 'At least we're going to have a pool. And apparently, there's a treehouse. Like, I can play my music as loud as I want up there, right?'

Theron's heart broke at Conor's words. He couldn't deal with this abandonment. His tone became incredulous. 'You're happy about it?'

Conor's eyes widened. He spread out his arms. 'I hate it. But hey, it can't be all that bad, right? And then when you visit me,' Conor's face reddened, 'we can bunk in that treehouse together.'

Theron felt himself tremble. Visit? He would no longer see Conor every single day, almost every single moment of his waking life. He felt like he was falling into a bottomless pit while the world around him shattered.

'You're abandoning me and you're happy about it!' Theron accused.

'Of course not!' Conor took Theron's hand in his. 'I don't want to leave you.' He rubbed his thumb on Theron's knuckles. 'Actually, I . . . Theron, I think . . . I'm—'

Theron thrust Conor's hand away. 'What kind of a friend *are* you to make promises to me about us never leaving each other's side and growing old together only to leave and act like you're excited about a stupid treehouse?!'

Conor gaped at Theron. 'Our friendship means *everything* to me.'

'Yeah right.' Theron sputtered angrily. 'You promised me we'd go to Prom together, just like at that dance, because our friendship was so strong, no one could come *close* to sharing what we have, not even a date.'

'Theron, that's because . . .' Tears sparkled in Conor's eyes. He whispered. 'We can still go to Prom together.'

'Forget Prom. In fact, screw it. Screw it *all* – you, this damn fake friendship. Because you obviously care more about a pool and a treehouse than you do me.'

Conor raised his voice. 'That's not true.'

Theron got right in Conor's face, seething. 'Then why are you leaving me? Why are you moving miles away? A real friend fights for those he cares for, and keeps his promises.' Theron spat his disdain, 'You're no friend. I thought you . . . cared about me, just as much as I do you, after I dedicated so much to you and *for* you. But you're like everyone else, caring about *things* rather than *people!*'

'Why are you saying these things?' Conor wept.

'You're not even fighting back.'

'What do you want me to do, huh?'

'Now I see your true colours. How you were just using me. Giving me false hope so that I'd do what you wanted and help you with your stupid! reckless! schemes!'

'Theron!!'

'Well, I'm done being reckless with you, Conor! I'm done being used and lied to.' He lowered his voice. 'I'm done with *you!*'

Theron turned to leave.

Conor grabbed his arm. 'Theron. Please, don't hate me.'

Theron stopped, feeling his heart shatter, for the love he felt – and the fear he felt. 'Enjoy that treehouse, Conor,' Theron said, voice trembling. 'At least you'll never have to hear me tell you you're being reckless again.'

Theron shoved Conor off him, turning away so Conor could not see his tears as they began down his face.

'Theron, please!' cried Conor.

Theron stopped. He turned and shouted tearfully. 'You used me all this time, didn't you?! Because you knew I'd follow you anywhere and get in trouble for you. And now you're leaving in just a week?! Good fucking riddance! I don't need your recklessness in my life. I hate it. I hate you! I never want to see you again!'

Theron spun and ran. Conor called after him, and Theron kept running. And when he got home, he dashed upstairs and collapsed onto his bed, realising the intensity of what he felt for Conor, just how much in love with him he was, and he sobbed as his heart broke again and again.

* * *

Silent tears streaming down his face, Theron stroked Conor's forehead, bringing him closer to his chest. He kissed Conor's brow, and whispered, 'Please be okay, darling.'

Theron closed his eyes. He heaved, exhaling a shaking weep, adrenaline draining out and leaving him feeling weak, the memories breaking his heart all over again, and his worry for his husband clenching it.

CHAPTER 6

Conor awoke to unfamiliar surroundings and he felt like he was even more out of it than he initially assessed.

The room he was in was sparsely furnished – he lay on a simple futon – and the room looked to have more traditional Japanese decor than what Conor remembered. The walls had an orange glow with dark wooden pannels accentuating them. The door was a sliding grid door with a simple lock; its mother-of-pearl sections appeared to be made of rice paper. And Conor recognised the woven mats as *tatami*.

Voices alerted Conor to Theron speaking with Kiyoshi and another man.

Conor tested his muscles, stretching. He ached still, and his head felt like it was in a vice, but his stomach told him he needed food.

Conor tentatively sat up and brought his legs to the edge of the futon, placing his feet on the *tatami* floor. He was no longer as weak and he realised he felt warm.

Pushing himself up, Conor made his way to the common area.

The three men stopped speaking and Theron's eyes widened, instantly glistening.

'Conor, darling, you're awake!'

Theron rushed to Conor, his tears already streaming down his cheeks as he took hold of Conor's face. The look in his eyes worried Conor as much as it moved him in all sorts of ways.

'I love you so much! You're the love of my life. And I am *not* done with you. I *need* you. I need your reckless-ness. I need you with me for the rest of my life!'

His last words were sobbed and it made Conor begin to weep. He cupped Theron's cheek.

'Babe. What's brought this on?' Conor recognised the words that were the opposite of the declaration that had broken his heart so long ago now. 'Why are you reliving that . . . ?'

'I'm so sorry for the words I said to you then. I . . . I think you were going to tell me you were in love with me.'

'I was trying to. Before you declared you hated me.'

Theron pulled Conor to him and held him so tightly, it frightened him. Conor reciprocated, weeping without understanding his husband's sobs.

'Babe . . . What's going on?' Conor pulled away, sniffling. 'Theron.' Conor creased his brows even more. 'I love you and I always will. You're the love of my life too. And I will never leave you. I will never abandon you.'

The two Japanese men remained silent, minding their business but glancing their way every now and then.

'Conor,' Theron began shakily, 'we were found at the safehouse and had to come to this hideout. I carried you, and protected you.'

Conor's heart clenched with love for Theron – and a jolt of shock at the realisation of what had happened while he was delirious with a fever.

'You were burning up, and I was so scared.' Theron choked out the words. 'They were shooting at us and Kiyoshi-san and Takuto-san got us out of there. And then you were mumbling the things you said back then, as though in your delirium you were reliving the fight I initiated because I had needed to break up for the hurt I felt at you leaving.'

Theron pressed his lips together before he let out another uncontrolled sob.

'Oh, babe.' Conor wrapped his arms around Theron.

'I was so scared you'd get worse.'

'Fever must've broken in the night. I . . . don't remember anything. Now I understand why I'm in a different place and . . .' Conor noticed their bags. 'Our bags?'

'Takuto-san retrieved them,' said Kiyoshi. He turned to the other man. 'Takuto-kun . . .' He spoke in Japanese.

Takuto nodded and brought Conor a hot mug of something that looked like coffee but smelled like anything but. He proffered the mug.

'Conor-san, this is *maitake* mushroom tea. Good for the immune system.' His accent was much thicker than Kiyoshi's, though his smile and eyes were very akin to his.

Conor accepted the mug. 'Thank you. You must be Kiyoshi's brother.'

The man bowed from the waist. 'Takuto. Thank you for saving my brother's life.'

Conor smiled. He wiped his eyes of any remaining tears as Theron continued to silently weep and shed a few more tears. Conor took his hand.

'I'm okay. A little lost and out of it, but I feel much better.' He took a sip of the tea and grimaced. The taste was a bit earthy, and the tea was pasty. But then a mild aftertaste of nuts replaced the woodiness. Conor contemplated it before taking another sip and began to enjoy it.

Theron chuckled. 'You get used to it. I already had my second mug.'

Conor widened his eyes.

'Conor-san,' said Kiyoshi, grinning, 'we are making real authentic Japanese ramen from chicken broth. Theron was telling me the two of you once stole dozens of ramen packets and almost got caught. This will taste much better than those packets that are a poor imitation of it. It will be good for you too.'

'Thanks. I appreciate it.' Then Conor added, 'Of course,' he grinned teasingly, 'you need me in shape to retrieve that clip drive.'

Kiyoshi chuckled. 'Yes, but I also need you well for . . .' He placed a hand over his heart and tapped. Conor understood.

Theron wrapped an arm around Conor's waist as the thief sipped the *maitake* tea.

'So tell me, do I need to call you Kiyoshi-san?' inquired Conor, having observed the exchanges and how Kiyoshi and Takuto both had addressed him. 'It's a title of respect, yes?'

'Yes. I do not oblige you to, but you are no longer clients,' explained Kiyoshi. 'You saved my life. You have my friendship.'

'Aw.' That warmed Conor's heart more than the tea warmed his oesophagus. He felt himself blush as fresh tears prickled his eyes, so moved was he at the evolution of his and Theron's relationship with their Japanese counterpart.

'You called your brother Takuto-kun when speaking to him,' observed Theron.

'Reserved for those closest to my heart,' said Kiyoshi.

Theron winked at Conor. 'Looks like we've still got some ways to go.' The four men chuckled.

Takuto returned to the steaming pot on the stovetop. He looked back at them as he gave his soup a stir. 'And the suffix is used only when addressing me directly.'

He nudged Kiyoshi and said something in Japanese, his wide smile infectious, even if Conor understood nothing of what he was saying. The two brothers laughed, their joy identical as they smiled fondly at each other.

'So where are we now?' inquired Conor.

'We are at a property an associate of mine owns in a small village. This associate has sent me much valuable information over the years. This place was our backup – only Takuto-san and I know of it.'

'And where is this associate now?' asked Theron, tensing slightly.

Kiyoshi placed a hand on Theron's shoulder. 'I know I can trust this person. Proven many times by the information sent that helped or saved our lives.'

'You speak as though you've never met.'

A smile curled on the corner of Kiyoshi's mouth. 'An observant detective. Rest assured, my associate knows we are here and will be joining us shortly.'

Theron nodded, seeming satisfied by that.

'The place definitely feels homely,' said Conor, sensing the welcoming peacefulness of the home.

'Oh, speaking of home,' said Theron, stepping away from Conor. Now Conor felt colder without his husband's warmth. 'Takuto-san did a sweep of our things in case of any bugs or trackers and,' he chuckled, 'we never removed Martha's tracker from your main outfit.'

Conor had completely forgotten about the tracker after nearly two and half years. He realised the implications.

Theron pulled out his phone. 'This came in this morning.'

Conor read the message Martha had sent Theron, trying to suppress a smile the whole time.

So you removed my tracker and rendered it useless. That's fine, but . . . WHAT THE HELL ARE YOU DOING IN FREAKIN' JAPAN?! Don't get arrested. Don't get killed. And don't forget to bring back some souvenirs for me.

Conor couldn't help but laugh. Then a dizzy spell hit him and he felt the room spin. Theron had his arms around him steadying him and a hand on the mug within seconds. He steered Conor to the sofa.

'Let's get you settled so you can rebuild your strength.'

As Conor sat down, he interlaced his fingers with Theron before the detective could step away. 'Theron, thank you for protecting me. And for being reckless with me.' Theron smiled fondly. 'For the record, I need to be a stickler too sometimes. I need you in my life too. Because you're the love of my life.'

Theron sat down beside Conor and leaned on him.

'I know whatever I was mumbling brought it all back for you,' said Conor. 'I'm sorry.'

'It's not your fault,' Theron relayed gently.

'You're my husband. We'll get through this . . . without getting killed, without getting arrested, and we'll grab something for Martha. But Theron.' Conor put the mug down on the coffee table and turned to Theron, cupping his cheeks with both hands. 'Thank you for always hunting me.'

'Thank you for coming back into my life,' whispered Theron.

Conor leaned forward and pressed a tender kiss to his husband's lips. He smiled, reaching for the mug and returning to his funny-tasting tea.

* * *

When the soup was ready, the four men sat down at the table to eat. Conor was served mostly broth with veggies, while the others' portions were more elaborate – there were noodles, thin meat, mushrooms, green onions, and other veggies.

Conor peered over Theron's bowl. 'Ooh, you have an egg.'

Theron chuckled, his heart still clenching. It wasn't just the memories that made everything feel so raw again, but the fever, the shooting. Everything right now was bringing it all back – the fight, finding each other, Theron's injury, thinking Conor was dying . . . The fear from the trauma of it all still lingered, even these years later.

Theron absently put a hand to the place where the dagger had protruded.

'Babe, are you okay?' Conor's tone and eyes spoke of panic.

'I'm fine,' Theron reassured. 'Just remembering every-thing we've been through. Sometimes I still feel the stab – ghost sensations.'

Conor nodded, lips pressed together.

Theron returned his attention to their hosts, who chatted quietly in Japanese while Theron and Conor had their exchange, not prying into their private affairs. 'This is delicious, Takuto-san. Thank you.'

Takuto bowed politely in response from his seat.

'How safe are we here?' asked Theron, the question still tugging at him.

'Safe. No one knows this place or our affiliation to it.'

'Except your mysterious associate you swear you can trust,' Theron said with a nod.

'What about the clip drive?' asked Conor.

'One of my men was captured and interrogated. They believe I sent him to find out the location of the drive. They do not know that their man whom they sacrificed told me its location. They will not move it.'

Theron pondered. 'Do you think he knew? The guy at the club?'

Kiyoshi shook his head. 'He would not have feared for his life from my knife if he knew a bomb would kill us both moments later. Shibuya purposely sacrificed his man without telling him. That is the nature of the man I am hunting.'

'Yeah,' Theron said, his voice low. 'He sounds like a real piece of work.'

The men finished their meal in silence.

The front door a few rooms away slid open as Kiyoshi glanced at his phone. 'My associate arrives.'

He stood to greet this associate, as did Takuto. Theron and Conor followed suit.

A woman perhaps in her sixties entered the room, clad in a traditional kimono that was at once simple as it accentuated her dark eyes. Her hair was speckled with silver, fine lines on her bronze face marking her sage years. Her smile was filled with warmth, and Theron immediately felt reassured. He felt safe, even though he did not know this woman.

Kiyoshi and Takuto gaped at the woman.

'*Okaasan!*' whispered Kiyoshi.

The woman's eyes filled with tears as she whispered. '*Musukotachi.*'

She opened her arms to both of them, and that's when Theron realised who this woman was. Conor must've realised it too, for his breath hitched with a quick quiet sob.

Kiyoshi and Takuto closed the distance between them and their mother, and she embraced them with the love of decades of caring despite the years apart.

She laughed tearfully, pulling away enough to grab Kiyoshi's face between her hands. She spoke some more before she did the same to Takuto. They embraced again.

'Kiyoshi-kun, Takuto-kun . . .' And her tone seemed to convey her love for her sons.

Theron found himself smiling at the reunion taking place before him.

Wiping her eyes, the woman turned to Theron and Conor and bowed. Theron and Conor bowed in return, conveying their respect.

She stepped up to them, beaming and said something in Japanese.

'My mother says she is very grateful for your actions,' Kiyoshi translated.

Theron bowed again. 'You're welcome. Uh . . .' He rose and looked to Kiyoshi for guidance. 'How should I address your mother?'

Kiyoshi exchanged a few words with his mother, a quick back and forth. Kiyoshi chuckled, turning back to the two Americans.

'My mother says because you saved my life, you may call her *Okaasan* too.'

Theron placed a hand over his heart. 'I am honoured, *Okaasan*.' He bowed.

'As am I, *Okaasan*.' Conor bowed too.

Okaasan beamed even more widely, her eyes smiling as much as her mouth. She took their hands in hers, clasping them. Her hands were warm, a bit rough on the fingertips, and her grip firm.

Then she turned to her sons again and her tone changed. It sounded like she was scolding them. The three Japanese family members argued with loving reproach, as *Okaasan* pointed a finger at her sons. Takuto lifted his hands in an exaggerated shrug as Kiyoshi gaped, shaking his head, the three of them talking over each other.

Theron blinked a few times.

Conor leaned towards him. 'Let's give them some space to catch up.'

They began to turn before Kiyoshi called after them. He took a few steps towards them and lowered his voice while Takuto and *Okaasan* continued their exchange.

'This has been a very . . . unexpected surprise. My mother has been my anonymous associate.'

'Always looking out for her sons, eh,' said Conor.

'Always.' Kiyoshi took a beat. 'She promises she has been safe. Her Intel . . . she will not tell us how she comes across it. She also scolded me for nearly getting myself killed.'

'That's what that was,' chuckled Theron. 'I can tell your mother loves you both very much.'

'Yes. We have much to catch up on. Please, make yourselves at home.'

'We might go for a stroll,' offered Theron. 'Allow you some privacy with your mother.'

Kiyoshi thanked them before returning to the discussion that had simmered down between *Okaasan* and Takuto who were now speaking excitedly.

Hands interlaced, Theron led Conor out and they strolled into the field. The setting sun was warm on Theron's face, even if the air had a cool touch. He looked at Conor, who must've detected his worry.

'I feel fine, babe.'

They continued for a bit and came upon a Japanese tree house that looked like it hadn't been used in a long time. It appeared inviting and cosy from the outside.

They both stopped, staring at it. Theron observed their surroundings – the home and a vegetable garden were enclosed within a small fence that included this treehouse.

As though knowing the question on Theron's lips, Conor voiced, 'Are you thinking what I'm thinking?' His pale blue eyes were earnest and it tugged at Theron's heart.

Theron took his phone and sent a quick text message to Kiyoshi, asking if the treehouse was *Okaa-san*'s and if he and Conor could explore it. The answer confirmed it was on her property and they were free to enjoy it as they pleased. Kiyoshi's phrasing made Theron's face feel hot as he relayed the message to Conor.

'Darling,' he breathed, his chest already heaving at the memories, the implications, and his desires. 'Remembering our fight, I recalled you saying you wished we could bunk together in the treehouse. So . . .' He smiled bashfully. 'Let's bunk together here, and forget for a moment all that's happened. Celebrate our belated honeymoon.'

Theron's smile widened as Conor beamed at him.

'Because I now know when you said bunk, you were hinting or probing.' Theron took both of Conor's hands in his. 'Conor, my love, my darling, I want to make love to you in this treehouse.'

Conor bit his lower lip, his cheeks flushing as he grinned at Theron. 'Then let's get up there and enjoy it *as we please* before I take you right here.'

Theron lunged and pulled Conor into a fervent kiss that left him needing more. Then he pulled away quickly, remembering his desire, and led Conor by the hand up the steps and into the treehouse. Giggling silly, they installed themselves clumsily before forgetting everything and losing themselves in each other.

CHAPTER 7

In the days that followed, Conor's strength and health returned. Kiyoshi and Takuto had several catch-ups with their mother, and while she left them to their talks with the two Americans without budding in, she had some information that would help and shared what she knew.

'My mother used to work in the plaza where the office building stands that serves as the headquarters for the *Nesshün'na Kōkan*. Thanks to her information, we know the adjacent buildings have good vantage points into the complex. She also informed me where the elevators and stairs are in that building. Should anything go wrong, we will have to move quickly. But should anything go wrong, Shibuya will be delayed due to the inconvenient positioning of the stairs and elevators in relation to the entrance.'

A wide series of glass doors served as the entrance – the elevators and stairs were said to be behind a large wall separating the main lobby from the secondary lobby. The complex itself was much taller than anything

Conor had ever scaled. Not only would he need a grappling hook, but also a climbing harness.

'My men have set up security cameras in the neighbouring skyscrapers. They will locate the room with the drive, locate the drive itself, and they will report with enough footage of the surroundings and roofs so that Vulpis can become familiar with the layout without the need to explore.'

Kiyoshi turned to Conor. 'Conor-san, will this be suitable for you to execute the mission?'

'Yes!'

And thus they gathered their footage for Conor so he would know the building's layout once he arrived on-scene, despite never having parkoured it.

Conor was on the comfortable couch while Kiyoshi and Takuto were in a conference meeting with other Yakuza. *Okaasan* had stepped out to visit a friend. Conor and Theron had helped her with the shopping earlier and she had made many snacks for them, which Conor had enjoyed, now wishing there were more.

Theron joined Conor and sat down beside him. 'What are you studying?'

'The layout of the skyscraper through which I'll be entering.'

'*You'll* be entering? You mean *we'll* be entering.'

Conor sighed, worried and wanting to keep Theron safe. 'Babe, it'll be safer if I enter alone. I need you with Kiyoshi and Takuto as backup.'

Theron stood abruptly and strode to the window. He spun around. 'No. I won't allow it. I'm going in with you and that's final!'

Conor rose and joined Theron by the window, cupping his face. He knew his husband wasn't trying to be authoritative but was merely frightened. 'I'll be fine,' he reassured. 'I need you to trust me.'

Theron shook his head, unrelenting his arguments. 'This isn't a question of trust, Conor. We don't have Martha's armour plating or bullet-proof padding. Should anything go wrong, should anything happen to you . . .'

The frantic fear in Theron's eyes broke Conor's heart.

Theron pressed his lips together, shutting his eyes tight. 'Then it'll mean,' he whispered. He turned his face away.

Conor's heart began to race with trepidation. 'Then it'll mean what?' He was so scared he knew the answer but was hoping Theron would prove his fear wrong.

'Then it'll mean that finding you and being with you was a mistake.'

The bitter admission stung, the reply worse than Conor had imagined. Conor let go of Theron with a jerk backwards, gasping. His chest tightened and tears stung his eyes.

'You don't mean that,' Conor managed, his voice a half-whisper.

Theron continued to stare away and at the floor. 'You can do what you want, *Vulpis*.'

Conor's breath caught at Theron's cold use of his thief name.

'As for me, I'll be returning to America.'

Theron stormed away and out of the home, slamming the sliding door shut.

Shaking with weak legs and feeling like his chest was being pressed down by a massive weight, Conor ran after his husband, calling his name. He was so hurt, so angry, and so scared.

'Theron, wait!' Conor caught up a few paces behind. 'Don't do this,' he implored. 'Don't do this again.'

Theron spun around and shouted. 'That's the thing, Conor. I *can't* do this again! I can't lose you, I can't bear to be abandoned by you. I would die! And take that stab wound a thousand times to keep you safe!'

Theron's tearful passion staggered Conor's heart, he heaved a shaking sob.

Theron spread out his arms. 'But we don't know that you'll be safe, that you won't die. And I am so scared right now that I wish I didn't know you.'

Theron turned and continued to stalk away.

For a moment, Conor felt like his heart was being ripped open. He knew Theron was terrified. But his words were so hurtful. Conor watched him go – like he had at 15. And then his legs propelled him forward.

Conor grabbed Theron, spinning him around, and wrapped his arms around him tightly. 'I let you walk away once and regretted it for fifteen years. I'm not letting you walk away from me again. I won't let you throw away what we have just because you're scared.' He wept more loudly, 'I'm not leaving you, Theron! I'm not abandoning you!'

'But you will if you die! We're dealing with dangerous mobsters!' As Theron shouted, Conor simply held him. 'Right now I hate your recklessness and wish I never knew you!' Theron's sobbed words were a torment. 'I wish you never walked back into my life! I wish Vulpis was in jail because then he'd be safe!'

Conor's chest was so tight with sorrow, he began to feel unable to breathe.

'I hate this! I hate that I love you this much that I feel this physically!' Theron jabbed at his own chest as he bawled his hurt. 'I feel physical pain from this fear, Conor, and I hate you for putting me in this position just for being Vulpis.' He screamed his last words hoarsely. 'I hate Vulpis! I hate *all* of this!!'

Conor took Theron's face in his hands. 'Look at me, Theron. Please! Look at me.' Theron squirmed in Conor's grasp, eyes meeting his. 'Please trust me. Please don't do this. Don't throw away what we have because you're scared.'

It took all of Conor's will to be strong for both of them, when he too wanted to have a meltdown because of his husband's hurtful words.

'I'm scared too. I'm scared to lose you too! Please, Theron, don't do this again, hate me and walk away!' Conor whispered a final tearful, 'Please.'

Theron contorted his face, struggling and failing to contain his tears. 'I can't!' He whispered, 'I can't do this right now.' He squirmed away, twisting out of Conor's hold. 'I am so scared, that right now I wish I didn't know you,' he repeated more gently.

Trembling, Conor stared at Theron.

'I need to be on my own, right now, before I say something more I'll regret.'

Conor ran forward again and caught Theron's arm. 'Theron! I won't let you walk away from me, from us, from this marriage.'

Theron shrugged Conor off him, storming away.

Chest so tight he could hardly breathe, Conor put a hand to his mouth as loud sobs escaped him, and he fell to his knees, watching Theron walk away, just like he had nearly eighteen years ago.

* * *

Theron returned after an hour. Conor remained silent as they all ate. Kiyoshi and Takuto attempted to prompt them into conversation to no avail. *Okaasan* also deduced what was up between the two husbands and attempted some cheerful prompts in Japanese to get them to smile.

Conor did his best to offer small smiles in thanks and small quick bows but their friends knew he was on the verge of tears.

Conor was still trembling. What more could he say?

Every time he met Theron's gaze, the man looked away. At least he was still wearing his ring – Conor supposed that was something. Yet, the archer on Theron's ring pointed his bow tauntingly at Conor's fox, their fingers feeling so far apart when all Conor wanted was to hold Theron in his arms.

Theron dismissed himself after a few bites before hunkering down in one of the rooms. Unable to remain at the table and control his emotions, Conor thanked their Japanese hosts and went to lie down in the adjacent room.

He curled in on himself, weeping. He could hear Theron sobbing, but Conor had not the will to go after him again only to be pushed away and told Theron wished he never knew him.

Clutching his wedding ring, his heart wrenching, Conor cried himself to sleep.

When he awoke, he became aware that strong arms held him – Theron's – and pressed him into the embrace. He felt pang after pang in his heart, remembering their shouting match from last night. Conor dared to look up into his husband's face, hoping Theron still wanted to *be* his husband.

Theron was sobbing as he held Conor. His face was inches above Conor's, his body protectively holding him, permeating such anguish and fear.

'Babe,' Conor whispered.

'I'm such a bad husband,' wept Theron.

That broke Conor's heart even more. 'No, you're not,' he tried to soothe, fresh tears stinging his eyes.

Theron's voice, wet with emotion, his face streamed with fresh tears pouring down his cheeks, looked deep into Conor's eyes, holding his face. 'I am *so sorry* I freaked out last night. You didn't deserve that. I am reckless to push you away when I'm scared. I hate myself for it. All I want is for you to be safe.' His face contorted in chagrin. 'You're the love of my life, Conor. I never want to lose you.'

'What you said hurt . . . a lot.' That was putting it mildly. Conor bit down any retorts he might have wanted to express – it would not help matters.

'I *do* wish that I didn't know you if you die, because it feels like my heart is being ripped open every time I think about what might happen. And then I see Lorenzo shooting you and the blood gushing from you, even if it turned out to be fake. I can't lose you, Conor.'

Conor placed a hand on Theron's face. 'Then we'll devise a plan so you can protect me to your best potential.'

Theron shut his eyes tightly, his tears falling on Conor's face, as Conor's tears streamed down the side of his temple.

'I love you too much,' wept Theron.

'You're not a bad husband,' Conor wept back. 'You're just as reckless as me sometimes.'

Theron stared into Conor's eyes, both men sobbing, and Conor felt Theron's love intensely, so much that it sent fire to his stomach.

Theron's lips were on Conor's as he sobbed loudly, claiming him, interlacing their fingers. Conor moaned a sob in response, deepening the kiss and opening his mouth to equally claim Theron for himself.

'Never leave me!' Theron demanded in a whispered sob.

'Never walk away from me!' Conor demanded just as tearfully.

'I promise.'

'I promise.'

And their love, desperate and passionate, culminated in a mix of mingling tears, wet kisses, sobs, and gasps of ecstasy.

* * *

Theron marched into the common room, determination replacing his earlier fear and anger. He locked eyes with Kiyoshi. This was a fresh day and it was time for a fresh attitude.

'We need to move in and get this over with. As soon as you give the go, Conor and I are ready to execute the mission.'

Kiyoshi rose to his feet. 'Good. Because I just received word from my men. Security footage confirmed the routine and patrols of Shibuya's guards. The room with the clip drive is left unguarded for only five minutes each night at the same time.'

'I can be in and out of there in three,' declared Conor.

Kiyoshi nodded. 'Then we drive into the city tonight.'

Chapter 8

Conor perched atop a high beam outside the sky-scraper. He readied his card-knife. Crouched where he was, he had a good vantage point into the terminal room but was out of view from anyone inside.

He remained calm, knowing Theron wasn't too far away if ever anything went awry. And this time, he was glad to carry a gun, well concealed beneath his satchel.

The mobsters within the room began to file out. Shibuya left last, setting a security system in the door. That wouldn't be a problem for Conor. If lasers activated, he could slink his way around, over and under them.

Finally, the door clinked shut.

'They're out. I'm going in.' Conor spoke in a quiet voice, knowing Theron and their two friends would hear him through their earpieces.

Conor leapt from his perch, grabbing onto the beam as he let himself dangle, knowing the harness would stop his fall if he slipped, and kicked out to land his booted feet on the window sill. He propelled himself forward, hooking the grappling hook for extra security.

It was much higher up than he was used to and he didn't want to risk a fall, even with these safety measures. Bruises were bound to happen on a job sometimes, especially when jumping or falling two or three – even four – storeys above ground. This . . . was something else.

Flicking his wrist, Conor aligned his cutter and sliced the window straight down, the stainless steel knife making it quick and smooth. He carved a rectangle before pushing the glass. It fell and shattered.

Conor waited a few beats to ensure no one re-entered, ready with his grappling hook.

Nothing.

Conor jumped in through the window, rolling and stopping in a low crouch. He observed the area. There seemed to be no lasers. He slowly rose, scanning his immediate surroundings before taking any more steps forward.

He clocked the computer that had been marked as the one with the clip drive and recognised the drive.

'I've got eyes on the prize.'

Conor hurried over and checked the computer to ensure the drive was indeed the one in question, not a fake. A few clicks into a folder told him his an-swer, as he recognised the *kanji* and *katakana* Kiyoshi had told him to look out for.

Conor pulled the clip drive out of the computer and secured it in his satchel. He turned, heading back to the window.

'I've got it,' he muttered. 'Heading back out.'

A loud click stopped him.

'Vulpis.' The voice was accented, silvery, and condescending. 'I should have known Kiyoshi would hire an infamous thief to retrieve the drive.'

'Shit, Conor.' The panic in Theron's voice tugged at Conor's heart. 'Darling, please be . . .' Theron stopped. *Careful? Cautious? Safe?* Conor knew all the thoughts whirling in Theron's mind, for those were the sentiments he felt for Theron too. They knew each other so well that they knew each other's minds.

Conor gulped, his heart thudding. 'I saw you leave the room.' He slowly peered over his shoulder, looking behind him.

'I looped back from another *hidden* entrance.'

Conor nodded, doing his best to control his breath – he felt on the verge of panic. He knew he had to think fast if he was going to get out of there alive. And right now, keeping Shibuya talking was his best bet.

Conor didn't move. 'I have to respect someone who knows how to sneak their way around.' He let his voice turn into a coo as he smirked. 'Another sly fox.'

The Japanese mobster gestured his gun at Conor and the thief understood to turn around. He did so slowly, lifting his arms in surrender.

The man was much older but well-kept, well-dressed, and muscular. If it came down to a fight, Conor was at a disadvantage.

Shibuya angled his gun to point at the desk beside Conor. 'Return the clip drive. On the desk. And I will let you leave with your life.'

Conor nodded once, slowly. 'Okay. I am going to get the clip drive out of my satchel.' He slowly moved his hands towards the satchel. His fingers closed around it.

And then he pulled up his gun swiftly, and shot Shibuya in the chest. The mobster fired as he staggered back but the shot went wide.

'Conor!' Theron shouted in his ear.

With no time to react to what had just happened – to what he had just done – and sending the image of the growing crimson blot out of his mind for now, Conor spun around and ran to the window, the adrenaline spurring his legs forward as his heart raced. 'I'm okay!' He grabbed the grappling hook and swung out of the window, letting himself slide down the rope enough to reach another rooftop.

'I'm out of there!'

Yanking the grappling hook back, Conor unhooked the harness, leaving the rope to fall behind him as he ran ahead, and jumped over to a balcony. He grabbed the railing, swinging his legs out as he let go, and landed on another balcony a few storeys lower. His knees buckled beneath his weight and he fell before finding his footing again.

Below, gunshots began to ring out into the night. Fear gripped him. 'Theron,' he murmured.

* * *

Theron felt like his heart was going to stop – his chest was so tight, it hurt him physically. And then Conor came into view and Theron could breathe again.

The door to the car to where the three others had retreated remained open until Conor leapt inside.

'Oh god, thank god,' heaved Theron, tears stinging his eyes.

Nesshiin'na Kōkan members continued to shoot at the vehicle as Takuto drove off, tires screeching. The mob-sters kept popping out from every direction.

Conor shut the car door barely in time to shield himself from a bullet that grazed the side of the car instead.

Theron levelled his gun, aiming it out of the rolled-down window, and shot one of the mobsters. A car gave chase, its engine revving as it drew closer.

Kiyoshi reloaded his gun and took aim from the passenger seat, shooting at the vehicle behind them. Another car emerged from an alleyway.

Multiple bullets hit the bulletproof rear window, each time making Theron fear the next shot would break through the glass.

Sticking his arm out of the window, Conor aimed out on his side, shooting at the other vehicle's tires, and the second car crashed into a dumpster.

'Conor-san!' exclaimed Kiyoshi. 'You killed Shibuya!'

'I . . .' Theron could see Conor's hands trembling.

Continuing to shoot with one hand, Theron reached over to stroke his husband's hand. 'I've got you. You did what you had to.'

'I've only killed once before,' muttered Conor.

'I know, darling.' Theron refocused on their pursuers. 'Let's make sure we make this job a success, yes?'

Conor nodded, and his face hardened into determination. The time to process the shock of it all would come later.

A bullet hit the rear windshield and the glass shattered. Conor yelped. Theron ducked, pulling Conor down with him. Thankfully the bullet had lodged into the thick glass.

Staying low, using the back of the seat for cover, Theron positioned himself to shoot at the mobsters behind them. Another bullet whizzed past his head. He cursed. He shot the mobster, killing him. A bullet hit something on the side of the car and Theron could smell leaking gas.

'Shit, we need to go faster or dump this car before it blows us up.'

Conor and Kiyoshi each killed another mobster, including the driver, but the man in the passenger seat took over. Theron took aim just as a bullet whipped towards him. He ducked out of the way, but not before the bullet reached his face. It gashed his left cheek and Theron cried out, feeling the sting of the burn as blood trickled from the slash.

'Theron!' cried Conor.

'I'm fine!' Theron's response was gritted. He refocused on their ever-pursuing enemy. The adrenaline was subduing the pain, though the pump of his heart was making it throb. Looking back quickly, he saw the bullet had lodged itself in the dashboard of the car.

Conor ducked lower. Takuto kept zigzagging the car, taking turns everywhere and anywhere, but their pursuer was relentless. The enemy's vehicle drifted closer, sidling up alongside theirs.

The *Nesshiin'na Kōkan* driver shot again and again, just as Theron, Conor, and Kiyoshi continued to shoot him in continuous streams as he dodged their bullets.

A bullet hit home, killing their pursuer, just as a thud told Theron the driver also shot one of them.

Breath shaking, Theron first snapped his gaze to Conor, who also snapped his gaze to Theron.

'I'm okay,' the thief reassured.

The car swerved uncontrolled and Kiyoshi reached the steering wheel, shouting out. 'Takuto-kun!'

'No!' Theron turned towards the front to see Takuto's head bobbing as blood drenched his shirt.

The car behind them crashed into a wall. Kiyoshi pressed on the brakes and their car halted.

The mobster placed his hands on his brother's crimson-drenched chest.

Takuto reached a bloodied hand to Kiyoshi and muttered something in Japanese. Then his head lolled forward. He was dead.

Theron swallowed hard – it could have been any one of them. Fear gripped him but it was no use. The smell of leaking gasoline invaded his nostrils and urgency took over.

'We need to get out of here before this car blows.'

Kiyoshi bowed his head, a few tears running down his cheeks as he continued to clutch Takuto's bloodied shirt.

'Kiyoshi-san!' shouted Theron. No reaction. 'Unless you wanna die too, we need to get out of this car *NOW!*'

Conor was already out of the car, and he opened the passenger seat, tugging Kiyoshi.

Then the mobster snapped out of it, his face hardening, and he leapt out of the car.

Taking hold of Conor's hand, Theron ran. Conor grabbed hold of Kiyoshi's hand, ensuring he followed. They were several paces away when the first burst of flames appeared on the car with a whoosh, heating their backs.

Theron urged his legs forward as fast as they could go. The three of them veered into an alleyway just as the car exploded, its blast deafening as it lifted off the ground and crashed back down.

Wincing and shuddering, Conor's eyes widened in shock. He reached for Theron who took him in his arms.

Theron felt blood trickle from his cheek to his jawline. He used his sleeve to wipe some of it. It was beginning to sting more prominently.

Kiyoshi's eyes were frantic – they were on fire as anger replaced his sorrow. He closed his eyes, turning his face away. Voice hoarse, he shouted angrily in Japanese, a series of what Theron assumed were expletives or profanities.

'I'm so sorry,' whispered Theron from over Conor's shoulder.

Kiyoshi shook his head before nodding.

Conor pushed away from Theron, a hand on his mouth and tears in his eyes. And then he ran a few paces, grabbing onto the wall for support, and bent, vomiting onto the pavement.

Theron winced. He walked over to Conor, and gently stroked his back. 'It's okay, darling.'

'I really don't have the stomach for this kind of thing.' Conor heaved, breathing heavily before rising and wiping his mouth with the back of his glove.

Theron took Conor's face between his hands. 'I've got you. We're safe now. We'll be okay.' He was trying to soothe himself as much as Conor. He pressed a brief but gentle kiss to Conor's mouth.

'I just puked and you're kissing me.'

'Yes.'

That got a small chuckle out of Conor.

Kiyoshi joined them, placing a hand on each of their shoulders. His face was grim. 'Conor-san, Theron-san, we must return to where it is safe. My men will clean these streets up. Shibuya is dead. His men will scatter until they can regroup. Thank you, Conor-san, for ridding this world of an abominable man.'

Conor turned to Kiyoshi. 'I just wish we could have done more to ensure they didn't take Takuto-san.'

Kiyoshi clenched his jaw. 'They paid the price.'

He turned and began to walk, wiping blood off his arm. Theron realised they all had minor injuries.

Hands interlaced, Theron and Conor followed Kiyoshi to the nearest safehouse.

CHAPTER 9

Theron hissed and winced as Conor gently cleaned the gash the bullet had caused on his cheek. Sitting facing his husband, he held Theron's chin gently, his hands stable despite his still shaking body.

'Almost done, babe,' he soothed.

Theron shut his eyes, letting out a quick groan. He breathed in sharply and then out, lips pursed.

Conor pulled the cloth away, dipping it to absorb more of the alcohol before dabbing it on Theron's face again. Theron held his breath.

'All right, now for the sutures.'

Theron took Conor's wrist as he pulled away, stopping him. 'Darling, how are *you* holding up?'

The question wasn't just about nearly dying, the job itself, or witnessing a friend die, it was also because Conor had killed – several mobsters.

'I'm okay.'

Theron cupped Conor's cheek, his eyes conveying what words could not. Conor leaned into his touch for a moment. He turned his head and kissed the palm of

Theron's hand. Then he noticed more blood on the gash and gave it another wipe in preparation for the sutures.

Conor expertly placed the dissolving adhesives on Theron's wound and applied the necessary glue. He smiled tenderly, leaning in and giving the gash a little peck – he felt himself blush as he pulled back.

'You're going to have a scar,' Conor said gently. Theron was racking up several now.

Theron offered him a wan smile. 'As long as you don't mind staring at my scarred face, I'm okay with that.'

'Yeah, you're handsome no matter what to me.'

Theron bowed his head. 'Had I moved a split second later . . .'

'Don't think that way,' Conor admonished, the fear gripping him anew.

'Barry's kidney donation would have been for nothing.'

'Theron!'

Conor placed his hand on Theron's face, on the cheek that wasn't wounded. Theron looked up at him, tears sparkling in his eyes. Conor placed his other hand over Theron's heart, feeling just how fast it was beating. He took Theron's hand and placed it over his heart so Theron would know he was feeling the same way, that his heart was thudding away just the same as his.

Conor motioned his head towards Kiyoshi. Theron nodded, understanding Conor's silent message – they had survived, there was no point in speculating about the alternative, because right now, Kiyoshi was grieving his brother's death and needed their emotional support.

The Japanese man was tending to his wounds in silence. He had remained taciturn since they left the scene.

They were in a penthouse suite now at a hotel the Yakuza owned just outside Osaka – owned by an allied clan.

Kiyoshi removed his shirt to dress a gash at the back of his shoulder where a bullet had grazed him, wincing and groaning as he dabbed on some alcohol. Conor watched in awe of the red and black Japanese dragon inked on Kiyoshi's back, spanning the width of his shoulder blades, its long serpentine tail curling in lazy eight loops.

Kiyoshi swivelled on the chair to grab more adhesives, revealing another large tattoo on his chest – a black silhouette with orange highlights of a phoenix, wings unfolding on Kiyoshi's pectorals. It looked like it was flying in for a landing, talons reaching towards the front, presenting a lotus flower on Kiyoshi's stomach whose black silhouette was highlighted with mild hints of purple.

Above Kiyoshi's breastbone, beneath his clavicle, was a small emblem, circular in appearance, all black, like a knot in a criss-cross with some squiggles and wings from what Conor could make out of it at this distance.

Around the Yakuza leader's neck hung a leather pendant with a round black gemstone that rested between Kiyoshi's pectorals. Conor wondered if that had a deeper meaning as well.

Conor knew that in Japanese culture, tattoos were more frowned upon than not. He didn't know enough yet about the Yakuza to know if these symbols meant anything to Tachibana Clan, but he knew enough about Kiyoshi to know that he would have chosen symbols that meant something to *him*. Conor would have to ask him about them at a more appropriate time.

Kiyoshi stood, buttoning his shirt again, and walked over to the small bar counter, taking a bottle of saké. He took three *o-choko* cups and carried it all to the couch, placing everything on the small glass table.

Conor and Theron joined him, sitting on either side of him.

Kiyoshi poured the saké into the cups and placed one in front of either American.

He raised his cup and solemnly voiced. 'To Takuto-san.'

'To Takuto-san,' Theron and Conor echoed.

Conor and Theron sipped their saké. Kiyoshi tilted his head back as he downed the drink in one go. He put a hand to his mouth, jaw clenching.

'It's okay to show emotion,' Theron reassured, placing a hand on Kiyoshi's arm.

Conor's heart broke for Kiyoshi.

Kiyoshi looked up at the ceiling, eyes red and blinking. 'We need to return to my mother. This is not something I want to tell her over the phone.'

'We understand,' said Conor. Set aside that they had left some of their belongings back at her place, he too felt that *Okaasan* deserved that courtesy and respect of mourning her son with the only child she had left.

Kiyoshi nodded, his face just as grim, his eyes hard with regret and anguish.

'You know,' said Theron, 'I never thought I'd consider you a friend, but here we are. I am so sorry for your loss. Takuto-san was a good man. He helped us and protected us and got us out of there alive. We owe him the greatest honour.'

Kiyoshi poured himself more saké. He muttered in Japanese and downed that cup too. He sighed, seemingly just a tad more composed. He looked at Conor expectantly.

Conor reached into his satchel and slapped the clip drive onto the glass table.

Taking the clip drive, Kiyoshi stood. He walked over to a laptop and connected the drive. 'Let us see what this can tell us.' He clicked around, searching the drive.

His face contorted in anger and he shouted in Japanese, hands going to his head. He pushed away, pacing.

'What is it?' asked Conor.

Kiyoshi pointed at the clip drive. 'Azumi-san was sold to a man named Hajime, and there is nothing more about her here.'

'Then we'll find this man,' asserted Conor, rising. He walked over to his friend. 'Kiyoshi-san, look at me.' Kiyoshi stopped pacing and met Conor's eyes. 'I am

Vulpis, the sly fox. And Theron is one hell of a good detective and hunter. We're going to find Azumi. We won't let Takuto-san's death be in vain. We'll find her. *I'll* find her. That's a promise.'

* * *

The following day, the trio acquired a vehicle and drove back to *Okaasan*'s village. They sat with her and held her as she wept for the loss of her youngest child. She had them promise to find Azumi and find out her fate. She also helped them locate this Hajime character.

They agreed it would be wise to take a few days to let their wounds heal before marching into this man's shop. It appeared he owned a warehouse for carpentry. The short rest would also allow Conor and Theron to enjoy the cherry blossoms in full bloom before any more fast-paced undertakings, which they appreciated.

They settled for the night. When Conor awoke, Theron was on the phone in the common room, shouting. Worried, Conor hurried to join him.

'But how the *hell* did that get in the news already and all the way to you!? . . . No, we're fine. . . . No. . . . We're after a slave trafficker. . . . I promise. . . . Martha!'

Conor stopped in his tracks, surprised. 'Martha?' He could hear her shouting now through Theron's phone, but couldn't make out her words.

'Yes, don't worry,' Theron tried to sound reassuring through the annoyance, Conor could tell. 'Okay, just a sec.' Theron pulled his phone away from his ear and put it on speaker. 'All right, we're all listening.'

'If you so much as *die*, I swear I'm going to find your bodies and kick your asses out into the next galaxy over! And this Kiyoshi?! You better keep them safe. They're already in hot water because you took them away – I had to vouch for them that they were coerced into mobster activity overseas.'

'Martha,' Theron warned, 'Kiyoshi-san just lost his brother. Please.'

'I'm sorry. I'm just . . . worried. Damage has already been controlled here – and mitigated – but I swear, my god, the two of you are so reckless.'

Theron chuckled. 'Yes, we are.'

'All right, gotta go. Stay alive! That's an order, even if you no longer work for me.' Martha hung up.

Theron showed Conor what had come in from Martha earlier. Her text read, *Explain this!* And a screen-shot of the article headline stated, *Notorious Thief-Turned-Detective Vulpis, Said To Have Killed Japanese Mob Boss in Osaka, Japan.*

Kiyoshi chimed in. 'I will keep you safe. My men confirm what *Okaasan* found about Hajime.'

'We can go in and question him,' said Conor.

'You're not going without me!' insisted Theron.

'That's why I said *we.*'

Theron pressed his lips together. 'I feel like hating you because I'm scared.' Conor took his hand. Theron added, 'I'm not walking away from this or from you. I won't push you away. I won't let you leave me.'

'Theron, it's okay,' Conor soothed.

Theron brought his free hand to his face and rubbed down, tracing his goatee. 'God, this is insane. I feel so many things right now. We need to retire, live a quiet life with Fidelis, do absolutely nothing.'

Conor smiled wanly. 'You think you won't get antsy? Can either of us manage that?'

'No, but I need to think we can,' admitted Theron. 'I need to catch myself when I want to . . .' He lifted his hand in defeat.

'I know.' Conor's tone remained soothing, all while Theron's tone was filled with torment.

'I get so scared.'

'I know.'

'You're the love of my life!'

'You're the love of my life.'

'And you will have that life of peace,' asserted Kiyoshi. 'I can do the rest alone. You can fly back to America. I will be fine.'

'No!' both husbands declared. Conor was surprised at the conviction in Theron's voice.

'We promised we'd help you find your sister. Takuto-san just died for us, all *three* of us. We're seeing this through to the end together, Kiyoshi-san!'

'Thank you, Theron-san.'

* * *

The trio of men stalked into the warehouse where a Japanese man in his sixties meandered about, carrying planks of wood. It was night out and they had ensured their quarry was alone.

'Hajime!' shouted Kiyoshi with authority and rage.

The man froze, dropping his wood.

With hurried steps, Kiyoshi marched to the man, grabbed him by the collar, and shoved him against the wall, making his demands in Japanese.

The man sputtered frantically in response.

Theron and Conor flanked Kiyoshi on either side, getting into Hajime's bubble as Kiyoshi got right in his face.

'You speak English?' Theron tested. The man nodded.

'My name is Theron Morin, detective. We're looking for a girl who was sold to you twenty years ago after she was kidnapped by the *Nesshiin'na Kōkan*. Azumi Tachi-bana.'

'Azumi Tachibana?' The man shook his head.

'Where is she?' demanded Theron. He unholstered his gun and leaned it against the man's chin.

Hajime made a few sounds of fear, wincing. 'Sold.'

'To whom?' Theron pressed, putting as much authority in his voice as Kiyoshi had in his.

Hajime responded in Japanese, fear in his eyes and voice.

Kiyoshi snickered in response. 'Kiyoshi Tachibana.' He paused deliberately. And spoke his next word slowly. '*Yakuza.*'

Hajime gulped.

'Do you know the name Vulpis?' Conor asked, his speech slow and voice filled with threat as he flicked his card-knife in his hands. Hajime's eyes widened. 'I am Vulpis. I killed Shibuya.'

'I suggest you answer our questions,' Theron went on. 'I don't think I need to tell you what the three of us are capable of together.'

Hajime nodded quickly several times.

'Good. Now talk! To whom did you sell Azumi Tachi-bana?'

Hajime blurted out his explanation in Japanese. Kiyoshi scowled.

'He says he was buying to resell overseas but the buyer's partner was an undercover cop and it was a bust. He stopped his operations shortly after.'

'Were the girls freed, then?' asked Conor.

Hajime nodded.

Kiyoshi scowled. He retorted in Japanese, to which Hajime replied. They went back and forth for a bit.

'Where did this undercover operation take place?' demanded Theron. 'Who was the cop?'

'Quebec. Marc . . . Jean-Talon.'

Kiyoshi shoved Hajime harder against the wall before letting go of him. He backed away and turned to go.

'Thank you,' Conor said in condescension as he turned. The Americans followed their friend outside.

Kiyoshi's scowl grew more pronounced. 'Why would she not return home?'

The question was one none of them could answer. Theron assumed she had either gone into protective care . . . or had died.

They walked back to the vehicle. Conor stopped before getting in. He shook his arms out a few times, 'Let's never do *that* again.'

'Agreed.' Theron caught his hand and interlaced their fingers. Such interrogations weren't his preference either.

Kiyoshi paused, hand on the car handle. 'Tomorrow, we fly to Canada.'

CHAPTER 10

Conor waited by the window just outside their quarry's firm. His office was an easy target – first floor. It offered a nice view – Conor could understand why he chose it. Getting in and out would be quick, which thankfully would give Conor more time to search the computer.

The detective must've been in his early fifties. Handsome features, as far as Conor could tell when the man turned his head to the side, silver hair that was long enough to look purposely dishevelled.

A young lady knocked on the door and then entered the office, speaking in French. Marc Jean-Talon answered and motioned with his hand.

From behind the secretary, Theron and Kiyoshi entered the man's office.

'*Bonjour,*' the man said, sounding jovial.

Theron nodded once. 'Hi. My name is Detective Theron Morin. I'd like to ask you some questions regarding slaves you freed some twenty years ago.'

'Ah, yes, *je vois*. My first success as an agent, back when I was doing undercover jobs.' Marc Jean-Talon leaned back in his chair.

Conor leaned against the wall, still peering in but careful to stay alert for any sudden movements that might indicate a need to withdraw so as not to give himself away.

'What would you like to know about the job?' asked Marc, his French-Canadian accent thick.

'Actually, we're looking for one particular woman,' explained Theron. 'You see, she was captured by a man named Hajime in Osaka, Japan.'

Marc nodded emphatically. 'Ah, the Osaka job. Yes, I remember when Hajime brought the girls to me.'

'We were able to trace the trade to you through Hajime, but then the trail goes cold. What happened to them after you freed them?'

Marc turned his head a bit. He was pursing his lips. He rubbed his chin – it looked freshly-shaved. 'Many of the girls returned home to their respective countries. Those who did not, chose to change their names. Some even remained here. They felt safer here than back home.'

Kiyoshi fidgeted, shifting his weight and looking at the ground. Conor could only imagine his deduction that his sister might have wanted a life free of the Yakuza.

Theron took a step forward and lowered his voice. 'I need to know if one of the girls still lives.'

'Who were you hoping to find, *Détective Morin?*' Marc pronounced the name as though it were French.

'A girl named Azumi Tachibana.'

The temperature in the room grew cold and Conor could tell Marc had stiffened. His shoulders rose slightly and his posture spoke of someone on alert, ready for trouble.

'May I ask *why* you are searching for this lady?' Marc's head movement told Conor his gaze had fallen on Kiyoshi. His tone was dangerous, and almost . . . protective.

'Please, I just need to know if she's alive,' said Theron, his tone reassuring but imploring – he must have picked up on Marc's body language.

Conor was beginning to get fidgety himself. He motioned with his hand to shoo them away and mouthed, 'Get him out of his office.'

It was clear to Conor that Marc would not give the information away, which was why Conor was out here, waiting to hack into the man's computer.

'All I can tell you is that she lives and has long since changed her name.'

Kiyoshi relaxed, closing his eyes for a brief moment in relief.

Theron took a beat. 'We need to find her.'

'She does not want to be found,' Marc insisted tersely. 'You do not have any official papers with you, or a warrant, so why should I divulge top secret information that this person went to great pains to keep from everyone but a select few? To keep secret from those in her country, including her family?'

Kiyoshi tensed at Marc's tone. 'I have been searching for her since the moment she was taken. Please, you have to help me.'

'And you are?'

Kiyoshi met the man's gaze. 'Her brother.' He bowed politely but quickly. 'Kiyoshi Tachibana.'

Marc rose slowly. There was a tense silence in the room. 'I heard the man who stole the girls for Hajime was killed in Osaka not too long ago.' His tone had taken on a defensive edge. 'That a thief named Vulpis killed him. And now, you come here in search of one of these girls.' He placed his hands on his desk, leaning forward. 'You may be a detective, *Monsieur Morin*, but my instincts never fail me. Kiyoshi Tachibana, you are *Yakuza, n'est-ce pas?*'

Kiyoshi clenched his jaw.

'With all due respect,' Theron interjected, 'my friend just lost his brother in the aftermath of a violent showdown while searching for his sister. He just needs to know she's safe.'

Theron placed a hand on Kiyoshi's shoulder. He placated Marc's defensive nature with reassurance. 'We understand you cannot divulge any information regarding her whereabouts. We just need closure, after all these years, after everything Kiyoshi-san has been through.'

'Kiyoshi-san! This man has your trust?' Marc seemed surprised, not in a bad way.

'Yes. I trust him with my life.' Theron adopted a more defeated stance, his tone searching to appeal. 'If you can just fill in some of the blanks as to what transpired after the girls were brought here so that my friend may return to Japan knowing the truth about his sister's fate. Perhaps over a coffee? On me.'

Marc's shoulders came down. Conor knew Theron had him.

'Very well.' Marc paused. His tone now was one of sympathy. 'I am sorry for your loss.' He walked from behind his desk towards Theron and Kiyoshi, motioning to exit the office.

Conor rolled away, leaning against the bricks, and waited until he heard the soft click of the office door closing. Then he faced the window once more, used his tools to wedge it open, careful not to break it, and lifted himself into the office. He had hacked into the computer within the second minute.

He had seldom needed his randomising hacking device, but it proved useful for deciphering passwords within mere seconds. The best part was, it looked like any other clip drive and functioned as one as well. Clipped to his key chain as it was, he always had it with him, and once again, it was proving invaluable.

Conor found what he was looking for amidst all the French he could barely understand. Then he hopped out of the window, closed it as best he could, and sprinted away from the building. He waited by the car for Theron and Kiyoshi to leave the small café and for Marc Jean-Talon to be far enough out of earshot.

The three men entered the car and Kiyoshi looked at Conor with earnestness in his eyes.

'Chantal Durocher. Works at a bar in town, here in Quebec City. I've got the address.' Conor held up the dual clip drive hacking randomiser.

Kiyoshi smiled. 'Thank you, Conor-san.'

Conor smiled back as Kiyoshi borrowed the drive to insert into his laptop. He entered the address into his G.P.S. before returning the drive to Conor.

'So what was the story our guy gave you?'

Theron answered as Kiyoshi drove towards the bar. 'Azumi changed her name, afraid to return to Japan because of her family being Yakuza. She became a legal citizen of Canada, learnt French, and was fostered . . . by Marc Jean-Talon himself.'

'Shit, that's why he seemed so protective of her.'

Theron nodded. 'Yup. He and his wife opened up a foster home to help the girls who wished to stay here.'

'It is noble of him,' voiced Kiyoshi. 'I am happy she had someone looking out for her when I could not.' They came to a red light. 'I wish she would have reached out to let me know she was alive and hiding.'

'Maybe she was afraid to,' Conor offered gently. 'Not that she was afraid of *you*, but of what might happen after living that trauma.'

Kiyoshi shrugged. 'It presented an opportunity for her to be safe and free from the life of crime. That is why I am not angry at her. I am sad about our circumstances.'

Conor and Theron both offered Kiyoshi smiles of sympathy. They remained silent the rest of the drive.

* * *

The three men stared at the building that was the bar. It was nondescript on a quiet street. Conor leaned forward, a hand on either front seat's headrest. Theron had to wonder if they had the right place.

An Asian woman with a light bronze complexion who appeared to be in her early thirties stepped out and placed a *Menu du Jour* folding chalkboard on the sidewalk. It was decorated with fun images of drinks drawn around the list. Kiyoshi drew in a sharp breath.

'It's her.' He placed a hand to his mouth, rubbing. 'She has grown so beautiful.'

The woman's long black hair fluttered in the wind as she arranged a few lights on the outside of the bar. She knocked on the window and the lights flickered on. She made a thumbs up, smiling to herself before returning inside.

A sign on the door lit up and it read, *Ouvert*.

Kiyoshi got out of the car, Theron and Conor following suit.

'So what's the plan?' asked Conor as they crossed the street. 'Ease into it? Blurt it out? I mean, do you think she's going to recognise you?'

'Darling, let the poor guy figure it out.'

Kiyoshi chuckled as he opened the door.

'*Bonsoir!*' Azumi smiled up at them as she placed a few coasters on some of the tables.

Kiyoshi froze. 'She doesn't recognise me,' he muttered lowly.

'Give her a chance,' Theron advised, matching his volume. 'We just walked in.'

Behind them a group of men entered, clad in black leather jackets, with motorbike helmets hanging at their belts. 'Hé, *Chantal, bébé.*'

Azumi sighed, deflating as one of the men sauntered to her. Azumi wriggled away from him before he could grab her arm.

'This just got interesting,' Conor muttered in sarcasm.

Kiyoshi was on alert, a hand near the back of his belt where he hid his gun.

'*J't'ai dit, Roger, de pu r'venir icite.*'

Azumi's tone was one of complaint, and her accent when speaking the Québécois jargon was as though she'd been born here.

Roger, a muscular man with a beard and tattoos, took hold of Azumi's arm, pulling her to him roughly – Azumi protested.

Kiyoshi was on top of Roger within seconds, yanking him off her and shoving him against the wall. Azumi's eyes widened. Kiyoshi pressed his hand on Roger's head as he pinned him.

'Touch her again and you're dead,' Kiyoshi threatened, his voice low.

The man lifted his arms in surrender. '*C'est beau, j'ai compris.*'

Kiyoshi shoved Roger away towards his companions, and turned towards them, cracking his knuckles. He drew himself to his full height, peering at the group of bikers with menace.

Despite them being more numerous and much larger in build, the narrowing of Kiyoshi's dark grey eyes and the sneer curling on the side of his mouth was enough to tell anyone this man alone was more dangerous than the six of them.

'*Àway, on sort d'icite. Estie!*' Roger turned and left.

Theron turned to Azumi. 'Sorry about that.'

Azumi chuckled. 'Thanks. I appreciate the help.' Her English was just as good as her French.

Behind her, a fellow bartender gaped at the trio. '*J'aurais pu m'en occuper.*' He shrugged.

Azumi pointed behind her. 'Étienne usually takes care of Roger.' The way both winked and smiled at each other told Theron the pair were an item.

Kiyoshi stepped towards Azumi. 'Does he bother you often?'

'Uh, no, I'm good, thanks.' Azumi downcast her eyes, looking uncomfortable as she tucked a strand of hair behind her ear.

Theron nudged Kiyoshi with his elbow. 'Less of the stern, more of the friendly.'

'My apologies.' Kiyoshi cleared his throat, his posture relaxing.

Azumi offered them a warm smile, and walked towards the bar counter. 'Can I get you anything? On the house for your help.' She reached over to grab something, her back turned to them.

'I . . .' Kiyoshi's voice cracked. He whispered. 'Azumi-kun.'

Azumi stopped. For a moment, Theron wondered if she had heard him. Then Azumi spun around, her eyes wide. She searched Kiyoshi's face. Theron saw the moment recognition dawned on her, and she gasped, bringing her hand to her mouth.

'Kiyoshi-kun?'

Kiyoshi nodded. Tears stung the siblings' eyes. Kiyoshi hesitated before reaching out with his hand.

Azumi ran to him and wrapped her arms around him. Kiyoshi returned the embrace, both of them letting their tears flow freely.

It felt like the walls had fallen and no years had passed since they had last seen each other. Such was the love the two had for each other.

Theron and Conor exchanged a smile of sympathy, taking a step back from the pair. They too were overcome with emotion as silent tears sparkled in their eyes.

Azumi pulled away, keeping her arms around her brother. 'Takuto-san?'

Kiyoshi's face twisted in chagrin and he shook his head. Azumi let out a high-pitched sob before burying her face in Kiyoshi's chest.

Étienne, from behind the bar, continued to prepare stacks of glasses and napkins, minding his own business, only every now and then glancing over his shoulder. His fond smile told Theron that he probably knew Azumi's backstory enough to be glad about the reunion.

When Azumi and Kiyoshi stepped away from each other, Etienne said something to Azumi and she nodded.

'Come, we can speak in the back.' She took Kiyoshi's hand in a familial clasp. She bowed her head before continuing. 'I feared you would be angry that I claimed a new life.'

'I feared you might be angry I came to find you so I'd know you were safe.'

Azumi let out a small laugh, and then the rest of their exchange was in Japanese as Azumi led Kiyoshi towards the back of the bar where a corner offered more privacy.

Étienne signalled Theron and Conor. '*Bière?*'

'No, thank you. We'll wait outside.'

Etienne nodded. Theron took one more glance towards his friend, where he and Azumi were weeping and laughing, holding hands and exchanging words at high speed. It was touching to see. And it felt like they could all finally relax, their journey and struggles had finally led them to Azumi.

Theron's breath shook with emotion. He felt Conor's soft fingers brush his. He took his husband's hand and they returned to the car.

CHAPTER 11

While they waited, Theron and Conor sat in the back of the car, diagonally facing each other. Conor entwined their left-hand fingers, looking down at their rings, the fox and archer meaning so much to him.

'Thank you,' he said gently.

Theron furrowed his brows. 'What for?'

'For following me. For hunting me. For sticking by me and staying with me.'

Theron's eyes conveyed sorrow at Conor's hidden implications. 'Darling,' he whispered, stroking the back of his fingers on Conor's cheek. Conor tightened their left hands' grip.

'Thank you,' Conor's voice cracked, 'for loving me and being my husband. I know all this, what we've been through, is all because I'm Vulpis.' Conor blinked back tears, his eyes never leaving the rings.

Theron gently tilted Conor's chin up so Conor would meet his gaze. His smile was tender. 'Conor, you're the love of my life, and always have been. I don't ever want to be without you. I'm sorry I freak out sometimes.' Theron squeezed their clasped hands. 'Thank you for staying with me even when I freak out. And for loving me even when I hurt you.' Theron bowed his head. 'I don't ever want to hurt you like that again. I promise to work on my fear-communication skills.'

Conor let out a small chuckle.

'I need you in my life. Always.' The conviction in Theron's eyes clenched Conor's heart and tingled him.

'I need you in my life. I've always loved you too.'

Theron suppressed a smirk. 'Martha says it took her and her husband at least a decade to get to a point where they had moved beyond all this . . . difficult stuff, but that even today they are constantly adapting and adjusting to each other. That this is normal, and eventually, it'll be second nature to reflexively not freak out.' Theron pursed his lips. 'She says as long as we are honest with ourselves and each other, our love can endure. There are compromises, sacrifices sometimes. I am grateful for all you've done to be with me the last three years since you came back into my life.'

'Of course! For you.'

'For you,' Theron repeated softly.

'And you never have to change, we just need to adjust to each other,' declared Conor.

'And I never want you to change. You are Vulpis and I love you for it. You're the reckless one.'

'And you're the stickler.' Conor grinned. 'Kiyoshi-san's right. We balance each other out.'

The two husbands rested the sides of their heads together, closing their eyes until Kiyoshi returned.

The Japanese man remained quiet for a moment. 'Azumi-san has a good life and is happy. She was glad I found her.'

'What's the plan now?' Theron asked gently.

'The longer I stay here, the more I put Azumi-san at risk. She has a life free of the Yakuza. She runs a good business, and has a good husband – Étienne.' Kiyoshi smiled fondly. 'We will keep in touch, in a safe and distant way.' Kiyoshi placed a hand on his heart. 'I am appeased now.'

Kiyoshi paused, and Conor and Theron waited.

'My brother's dying words were, "Find our sister. Tell her I love her, as I do you."'

The revelation brought a wave of emotions to Conor's heart.

'I did that now. I have honoured Takuto-san's wish.' Kiyoshi turned his head to the two husbands. 'Now we fly back to your city.'

'You'll stay with us for a bit, yes?' inquired Theron.

Kiyoshi merely smiled, beaming, before starting the car.

* * *

When the jet landed, the three men stepped out; Theron and Conor were carrying their suitcases. Kiyoshi stopped several steps later, his face relaxed but grim.

Theron and Conor turned to him, noting the lack of luggage.

'You're not coming with us, are you?' Theron deduced.

Kiyoshi smiled apologetically. 'I must return to Osaka. There is much to take care of in the aftermath of everything that's happened.'

'We understand,' voiced Conor.

Kiyoshi furrowed his brow. 'Conor-kun, Theron-kun, thank you for everything. You are ever in my heart.'

Conor noted the change in how Kiyoshi addressed them, and the meaning of it moved him to tears.

Theron reached Kiyoshi first, embracing him tightly. Conor joined the group hug.

'You're in our hearts too, Kiyoshi-kun,' Conor proclaimed. He backed away, wiping a tear, and laughed at himself.

Kiyoshi took each of their hands. 'If you ever need help – for *any* reason – you need only call me and I will fly to you, my American brothers.'

Conor heaved shakily. 'Oh my god,' he whispered, hiding his eyes. Kiyoshi chuckled, his voice wet with emotion though no tears escaped his eyes. When Conor looked up, Theron was also weeping, tears trickling down his cheeks.

'We've been through so much together, haven't we?' Theron stepped back too, joining hands with his husband.

'We have.' Kiyoshi bowed from the waist, a deep, low bow of great respect.

Theron and Conor bowed as well, deep and low to convey all that they felt towards their Japanese comrade. Chuckling and weeping, the husbands gave Kiyoshi another hug before backing away from him.

'Be well, you two. Take care of each other.'

'We promise we will,' said Theron. 'Kiyoshi-kun? Thank you, too, for everything.'

The three of them took another moment to merely smile at each other and allow the emotions to pass between them, however each was reciprocating it. Then Kiyoshi turned back towards his aircraft.

Theron and Conor watched Kiyoshi enter the jet, and remained on the landing strip until the plane was high in the sky.

* * *

The return home was bittersweet. Theron felt melancholy as all the adrenaline escaped his body, and all he wanted to do was curl up with Conor and Fidelis and take a long nap.

Barry was pleased to see the pair, who thanked him, Conor doing so profusely as he wrapped his arms around Fidelis, patting and stroking her mane.

'Don't thank me yet,' Barry chuckled as he left.

Theron collapsed on the sofa, Conor beside him, and they dozed off, with Fidelis sprawled on both their knees. When they awoke, they putzed around. It felt strange to be back to normalcy after everything they'd lived in Japan.

Theron had just stepped out of the shower when there came a knock at the door. He quickly dressed and went to answer.

He was surprised to see who stood on the other side.

'Oh, uh, Theron? My, you've grown handsome.'

'Mister and Missus Robertson!' Theron merely stared at them as they hesitantly stared back.

Conor joined Theron at the door. 'Mom? Dad? What are you doing here?' His tone was of surprise, not anger.

'Well, you see,' began Conor's dad, Stephen, wringing his hands together, 'your friend Barry called us from your phone—'

'Barry hacked into my phone?' Fidelis sidled up at Conor's feet, wagging her tail and looking up at the newcomers with curiosity.

'Something about our son being kidnapped by Japanese mobsters and if he makes it back home, well, best we mend bridges before losing him forever.' Nancy, Conor's mother, looked like she was relieved to see Conor alive and well.

'That's Barry for you,' said Theron, now understanding Barry's parting words.

'I . . . We lost a friend in Japan,' said Conor. He shuffled his feet, kicking at the welcome mat as his gaze dropped to the floor. Theron remembered Takuto's sacrifice.

'Barry told us you got married,' said Nancy.

'Yeah, I did,' asserted Conor, his tone a bit on the defiant side as he looked up again. 'To Theron.'

'Yes, Barry said as much. I suppose we are glad it's him, if anyone.' Stephen rubbed his chin. 'I mean, you used to tell us all the time you were going to marry him. We had thought it a phase. Though I suppose Theron did always keep you more on the straight and narrow. Oh, uh, well the . . . you know.'

Stephen's nervousness was something new, and the way he became self-conscious told Theron he was making an effort.

'What your father's trying to say is that while we might have . . . had difficulty in the past accepting your sexuality, we're happy you are with Theron. He was always such a good boy. We know he'll be good to you.'

'I suppose that's something,' muttered Conor.

Theron glanced over his shoulder. 'Would you like to come in?' If neither Conor nor his parents were going to make the next step, Theron might as well.

'Uh yeah, you can come in.' Conor stepped aside. His parents entered, their bodies rigid and movements awkward as everyone settled in the living room.

Before they sat down, Stephen sized Theron up and down. He'd always been a stern and intimidating man, and Theron felt like a child about to be scolded. 'You taking care of my son, yes?'

'Uh, yes. I . . .' He felt very scrutinised and uncomfortable all of a sudden.

'Good. Else we'd have words for you. If my son is to be with a man, I want it to be with someone we feel is good for him. We've always liked you when you were little, kept Conor from getting into trouble. Now I hear he's this Vulpis thief, and you're a detective. I . . .' he turned to Conor, 'accept . . . that you are married to Theron.'

Conor's eyes glistened. 'Do you accept that I'm gay?'

His father worked his jaw. 'I accept that you love this man.'

There was an awkward silence. It wasn't the answer Conor was hoping for, Theron knew, but it was much better than what they had both feared.

Theron motioned towards the couches where the four of them sat down.

'Your father and I have been going to classes to better understand the . . . LGBTQ community.'

Conor's eyes widened. 'For me?'

'Of course! You're our son, we love you.' Nancy bowed her head. 'We're both terribly sorry we gave you the impression we did not when we . . . failed to understand your sexuality. We want to do better. We may have our beliefs, but you are still our son.'

Conor brought a hand to his mouth as tears spilled from his eyes. 'I love you too, Mom, Dad. I just . . . When you asked those questions and believed it was a phase, then tried to help me meet girls, I just . . . I thought you'd never accept who I am – *how* I am. I know you cared in your way but . . . Thank you for respecting my space when I needed it.'

Nancy nodded, tears in her eyes. Another moment passed.

'It's commendable of you to step out of your comfort zone to broaden your understanding,' expressed Theron, subtle tears making his eyes moist. 'Not many who are as set in their ways are willing to do that.'

'It took us long enough to realise the problem was not that Conor was gay but that we had little understanding of what it meant for him to be gay.' Nancy reached a hand over to Conor. 'Do you forgive us?'

Conor nodded, unable to reply. He pulled his mom into a hug and his dad joined in. Nancy reached for Theron to join them, and the four remained in a group hug for several long minutes.

When they pulled away, Stephen cleared his throat. 'I'll be honest, I still don't get it. My upbringing was very rigid and still today I abide by many of those beliefs. That being said, while I had an idea of Conor marrying a woman to form a family of his own, looking back at it, his family always included you, Theron. I always considered you a second son. So,' he inclined his head forward and met Theron's gaze – this time not in intimidation, though still commanding. 'I accept you as my son-in-law.' He paused, brows furrowing in thought. 'You *are legally* married, yes?'

'That is correct,' said Theron.

'Good.'

Theron nearly laughed. He was nervous and relieved at the same time. This was strange, to say the least, but Conor relaxed as they recounted their trip and introduced Fidelis.

Nancy pulled out a large binder from her bag. 'I brought some childhood photos.'

'Oh my god, for real?' Conor seemed excited.

'I told your mother it would only embarrass you, but she insisted that since Theron is in almost all of them, it wouldn't be *as* embarrassing.'

'No, I want to see them!' insisted Conor, leaning towards his mom to look at the pictures within the binder.

'*I'm* the one feeling embarrassed.' Theron felt himself blush as Nancy showed them some pictures of the two boys as kids – they were holding hands in most photos.

'Look, here, you're kissing his cheek!' Nancy whooped a laugh.

Theron chuckled as Conor flipped through more pages of photos, sitting close to his mother, pointing at every picture he commented on. Theron's face felt so hot, he wanted to hide.

'Aw, look, babe, you're holding my face, and we were just ten.'

Eventually, they came to the photos of the school dance.

'You both look quite dashing in that one. I approved of your suits.' Stephen chuckled,

'We danced at that dance,' said Conor. 'As in, together. A slow dance.'

Stephen narrowed his eyes at Theron. 'That dance was shortly before we moved. Conor cried for weeks because *you* claimed you hated him.'

Theron shrank under Stephen's glare.

'If I accept my son's husband, you must promise me never to break his heart like that ever again.'

'Yes, sir.' Theron's voice was small, he could barely meet Stephen's harsh gaze.

Then the man grinned and chuckled. 'Good. I can get behind this. I am uncertain how I would have accepted any other man as my son-in-law.'

'Pressure's on, then, eh?' Theron combed his fingers through his hair. 'Conor is the love of my life and always has been. It took us too long to realise it and to admit it.' Theron put all the love he had for Conor and conviction in his voice. 'We're never letting go of each other again. I was Vulpis's hunter – Conor's hunter. I am never letting my prized catch get away again.'

'Babe,' Conor suppressed a laugh, widening his eyes.

Theron puffed out his chest. 'I mean it. Darling, I love you. And if your parents accept *me* as your husband, I want them to know I will be the best husband you could ever have.' Theron's heart quickened. 'I don't want them to want or accept any other man for you, because I am the *only* man for you.'

Conor's face went from surprise to touched, to something else, and he bit his lower lip, grinning, looking up at Theron from behind his eyelashes. That made Theron feel all sorts of tingles in his stomach and elsewhere in his body.

'We accept you and Theron together because we've always cared about Theron too,' voiced Nancy. 'After you wrote to us and we started going to those groups, we thought back to Theron. When we learnt from Barry you were married together, we started with that to accept you more. We may have our convictions, but we are trying.' The vulnerable honesty in her voice was endearing. 'I was so scared – *we* were so scared, hearing about the mobsters . . . When Barry called us to tell us you had returned home, it felt like I could breathe again.'

'Yeah, we know that feeling too, Mom.'

They shared a smile as understanding passed between them, something unspoken that finally all four of them simply knew and felt.

'And you're gay too?' Stephen asked Theron.

'I am bisexual.'

'And you chose Conor, you chose my son?'

'I love him, I always have and I always will. I was with others, but . . . He's the one for me. None made me feel what I feel for your son.'

'It was the same for me with any other guy,' said Conor.

Stephen and Nancy asked more questions, some borne from curiosity, others from their beliefs and ignorance, but it wasn't the kind of judgemental ignorance Theron would have expected after having heard some of the arguments Conor had once had with his parents. They truly *had* made an effort to better understand, and to accept their son, so that they could mend bridges.

They were honest, as were Conor and Theron, but the conversations were open-minded. Conor asked about his parents' beliefs growing up, wanting in turn to know why they had judged him previously. Theron knew it would take more to fully reconcile, but he was glad they could enjoy some time together like this. He was pleased Conor's parents were willing to learn from their son, not lecture him but share where they came from, so he and Theron would know, not as an excuse but as backstory.

After a few hours and after having shared some snacks, Stephen and Nancy left.

* * *

Theron and Conor leaned into each other on the sofa, contemplating everything.

'How do you feel, darling?'

'That was . . . the most . . . heartfelt conversation I've had with my parents in, like, forever.' Conor sighed. 'I still don't know that they fully accept me being gay, though.'

'They're willing to understand,' Theron reminded him, his voice tender. 'They are happy we are married.'

'Yeah, but not that I married a man, that I married *you*. Good to me and good for me, they kept saying.'

'It's a start in the right direction.' Theron interlaced their hands.

Conor smiled. 'They've always adored you.'

'I keep you from being too reckless.'

'And I keep you from being too much of a stickler.'

They both chuckled.

'You're right,' Conor went on. 'They're putting in the effort.'

'Your mom and that photo album,' laughed Theron. Conor laced his hands behind Theron's neck and Theron did the same as they faced each other.

'I need a bit of grounding from time to time,' admitted Conor.

'And I need a bit of adventuring.'

They smiled tenderly at each other, leaning forward, lips almost touching.

Conor bit his lower lip. He spoke softly, 'I love you, Theron.'

'I love you, Conor.'

The thief and his hunter kissed, impassioned, and melted into each other.

Not the end.

The thrills of the thief and his hunter continue in the
new trilogy, *Vulpis*.

*Conor and Theron's lives are thrown into shambles
when an insidious agent blackmails Conor into helping
one of the most abhorrent mafias to exist.*

<u>THANK YOU SO MUCH FOR READING</u>

If you enjoyed this story,
please consider taking a few moments
to write a review on Amazon or Goodreads.
It would mean so much.

Thank you.

Eidahs is a pseudonym for all mature written works, from thrillers to erotic romance. Eidahs in pronunciation sounds elven in nature, which is why she chose it, to tap into her love of fantasy, a genre that couples well with super-natural and preternatural, dark fantasy, and romance.

Eidahs is also the nickname 'Shadie' backwards, representing the shadow self, innermost desires, and a spectrum of emotions, most notably, passion, sorrow, rage, and delight, which Eidahs loves to incorporate in her writing. Enticing readers and evoking the characters' emotions when she writes has guided her inspiration to spell many short stories on Medium and a series of books under this pen name.

Connect with Binky Ink:

WordPress Website & Blog
   https://binkyproductions.com/binkyinkwriting
Medium – Main Profile
   https://medium.com/@BinkyInkWriting
X (Twitter) https://twitter.com/binkyinkwriting
Inkitt: https://inkitt.com/eidahs